break my fall

JESSICA SCOTT

Printed in the United States of America
First Printing 2016

ISBN: 978-1942102144

Author photo courtesy of Buzz Covington Photography
Cover Photo courtesy of Reggie Deanching
Cover design by Jessica Scott
For more information please see www.jessicascott.net

DEDICATION

This book is not dedicated to my husband.
For obvious reasons.

ALSO BY JESSICA SCOTT

FALLING SERIES

Before I Fall
Break My Fall
If I Fall (Forthcoming)

THE HOMEFRONT SERIES

Homefront
After the War
Forged in Fire

NONFICTON

To Iraq & Back: On War and Writing
The Long Way Home: One Mom's Journey Home from War

break my fall

Chapter One

Josh

How about you spell 'hegemonic'?" I didn't come to The Pint tonight looking for a fight. I swear to God I didn't. I am trying to behave.

But I don't belong here. Not tonight. Tonight, The Pint belongs to the perky college girls spending Daddy's money before the semester starts and the frat guys figuring out how to get laid.

Or guys like this fucking tool in front of me who think that evil people in the world can be reasoned with.

All I wanted was to have a beer and bullshit with Eli and the guys who knew what it meant to eat dirt in Iraq and instead, I'll start my second semester just like I ended the first—in a damn bar fight.

Because there's just something about the phrase American hegemonic empire that sets my blood on fucking fire, and when it comes from this smug little know-it-all Marxist in the middle of a gentrified part of a tobacco town...let's jus say my PTSD is flaring up.

This isn't going to end well. Of that, I'm reasonably certain. And I won't apologize for that, either. Anyone who tells you fighting isn't the greatest feeling on earth has never felt the fucking rush that violence brings.

Part of me welcomes it. The feeling of fist pounding into flesh. The pain.

The pain is the only thing that's real anymore.

Another part of me, though. Another part burns with shame at the anticipation flooding through me.

I square up with the cocky little fucker who thinks he's being ironic wearing a Kermit the Frog t-shirt.

"I'm all set, Colonel Jessup," the hipster says.

I lift one eyebrow. "You realize that's not an insult, right?" People misunderstand Jack Nicholson's character from A Few Good Men. They think Colonel Jessup is a monster. He's not.

He's doing what his nation asked of him. Defending it. Guarding it against the wolves that prowl outside the door.

Call it patriotic bullshit if you want to, but there are bad people in the world. Pretending they don't exist or that they just need jobs or pussy doesn't make them any less willing and capable of hurting the people I care about.

But I'm not at war anymore. At least that's what I keep telling myself every day when I wake up and remind myself that I'm home. It's what I want to believe when I don't see military vehicles rolling through desert sand on the 24-hour news.

Sometimes, I think I'd rather be there than here,

dealing with this dickbag who thinks he knows how the world works because his professor told him about it.

He takes a sip of craft beer and tries to look disinterested. "The fact that you can't determine when you've been insulted isn't my problem." He waves a hand in my face. "Go back to murdering civilians in Afghanistan or something."

And there goes my rational thought.

To be honest, I'm not sure if I'm about to get my ass kicked today or not, but that's not really what I'm thinking about when I snatch his craft beer off the bar and throw it in his face. Eli is going to kill me for the seventh time this month for fighting again.

One of these days, I'll show up to a fight when my opponent has brought a gun or a knife but I'll worry about that when the time comes.

Slam. Another fist, this one to my jaw because I'm not paying attention. His shithead buddy charges me like a fucking bull, and before I know it, we're crashing into the front door. It doesn't break. I don't think.

Still. Eli is going to kill me.

We crash into the street, and because it's a Thursday night, it's busier than if it was Monday. I'm vaguely aware of strong hands yanking me off him. And then I'm not thinking. I'm fucking pissed because this was supposed to be between me and the hipster and now it's not.

The hipster's buddy is on his hands and knees. I think that's a tooth in the pool of blood.

Strong hands slam into my chest. "Jesus, man, do you have to do this every night?"

Eli. I spit blood onto the sidewalk and swipe my hand across my mouth. I am aware of everything around me. And I can really feel. Every heartbeat. Every nerve. Every pulse of blood out of my body and down the side of my face.

I feel alive.

Except where it counts.

"What's the damage?"

"It's not about the money, Josh." Eli is my height with black hair and a beard he claims is his reward for having to shave every day since he turned seventeen and decided that joining the Army would be a fun way to see the world. Except that he did it the hard way and went through West Point.

Isn't that why we all joined? Oh wait; war. That was the thing we all joined for. At least, I did.

Eli is remarkably well adjusted for a West Point officer.

I look around at the crowd that's starting to dissipate. Now that the fighting is over, there's nothing more to see. Too bad these spoiled little fucks don't know what living really is. Worst thing they've got to deal with is too much homework and whether Mommy and Daddy will give them extra money so they can afford to buy Adderall from their dealer to stay up all night "studying".

You'd think I would be too young to be this jaded and cynical. Oh, but I wish that was fucking true. And right now, I'm not overly interested in unpacking any of it with Eli.

I just want to drink.

I fling my arm around Eli's shoulder. "So what's on tap for the rest of the night?"

But apparently, I was right about him wanting to kill me. He jams a finger into my chest. "You know what? I'm really getting tired of running defense for your angry veteran bullshit."

We've been down this road before. He'll bitch at me for fighting, I'll tell him I'm working on my anger management techniques—which we both know is a lie—and we'll go back into his bar and throw a few back. Sometimes a couple of the guys from the b-school will join us but most of the time, it's just me and Eli after things shut down.

"Get some ice for that eye and go home. I'm done tonight."

I drop my arms, the adrenaline starting to fade. "What the hell crawled up your ass?"

"Nothing. I'm sending you home before you start some shit with the next guy who decides to look at you cross-eyed. One fight per night limit."

"New rule or something?" I try to grin but pain starbursts through the side of my face.

"Just...take some ice and go, Josh." Eli sounds tired.

I offer a mock salute and flinch when my fingers tap the edge of my swollen eye. My fingers come away sticky.

Blood. Huh. I guess I'm used to it. I suppose it means I'm alive, so there's that.

I walk into Eli's bar and grab a towel and stuff it with ice. Drop some cash on the bar to cover my tab and head out. I step into the street and dab the towel on my eye. Shit that hurts.

I pull it away and look down at the towel. There's a lot of blood.

Well, fuck.

Abby

I'm generally not afraid to walk home from work at night. I walk through campus to my apartment on the other side of the sprawling buildings and new construction.

It's my way of fighting the fear that would paralyze me if I let it.

But I refuse to let my past define my future.

I'm stubborn that way.

But tonight, apparently, my little act of daily defiance against the world might turn out to be a bad decision.

I'm only a block from my apartment. I'm on a well-lit sidewalk.

So why is the hair on the back of my neck standing up?

I'm not overreacting. I rarely do. I'm pretty good at feeling when the shit and the fan are going to make babies.

But somehow, I missed the part when the two

drunk guys stumbled out of The Pint, singing some bastardized off-key song that's so badly mutilated, I can't tell what it is.

I walk a little faster. Hoping I'm invisible. I usually am, unless someone decides they want to fuck the black girl. Then I get noticed. I fucking hate feeling like this.

And because my life is a series of clichés no matter how hard I try to pretend otherwise, the shorter one sticks around when his buddy ducks into the alley.

"Hey baby."

Damn it. It's always the little ones you've got to worry about. Them and the gym rats who get juiced on steroids.

Head up. Make eye contact. Don't look weak or intimidated. "Not interested."

He frowns. At least I think he does. He's hidden in a haze of Ralph Lauren-wearing nightmares.

He steps in front of me. "That's not very nice."

Chin up. Hope he doesn't hear the fear in my voice.

"What's your name?"

"None of your business."

Yeah, I'm being rude. But I learned a long damn time ago that you never, ever show weakness in situations like this. My friend Graham would tell me to stop antagonizing the situation, to de-escalate it. But I'm not wired that way. I hate feeling weak. Guys like this will back down if you offer a show of force.

Usually.

My heart is in my throat.

"You're not being very sociable, honey."

"Hey."

Mr. Ralph Lauren looks over my shoulder. I can't not look.

It's just not my lucky day. I'm trapped. Never really figured on this as a possible end to the night.

This is what I get for not paying attention.

"I think the lady said no."

I stiffen at the voice that melts out of the darkness behind me. And as I glance over my shoulder, I hope to hell things didn't just get worse.

They definitely just got interesting, though.

My idea of a hero is not a big, muscular guy sporting week-old scruff and holding a bloody bar towel to the side of his face. The rational side of my brain isn't working really well right now, but I need a way out of the jam with Pink Polo and this might be it.

Pink Polo shirt holds his hands up. "Why the hell do you care?"

"Maybe because I said I wasn't interested," I say. I don't know how to do this. How to stand here and let someone else fight my battles for me.

Pink Polo drags his eyes down my body and back up. I feel naked and exposed and alone.

Big guy comes to stand next to me. And, oh god, why do I notice that he smells good? Like smoke and sweat and spice. "Take it somewhere else."

Maybe it's adrenaline. Maybe it's fear.

I don't know and I damn sure don't know how to

deal with any of the crap that's happening tonight.

But for a moment, I am not alone. For once, standing in the darkness, someone is standing with me.

It is an utterly unfamiliar sensation.

Pink Polo spits on the pavement. "Fuck you, man. She's not worth it." He slinks off, looking for his buddy.

My throat relaxes, just a little bit, and I can finally take a deep breath.

And then I get another good look at my hero.

For a moment, I'm fixated on the side of his face that he's dabbing with a towel. The blood distracts me, but only for a moment.

His dark eyes are locked on me and suddenly, I no longer notice the blood or the bleeding.

"You okay?" His voice is thick and gritty, his words clear. Like he's not standing there, actively bleeding.

Wring your panties out, ladies.

I swallow and nod. There is something familiar about him that I can't shake, but now is neither the time nor the place to start digging into that, no matter how much I might want to. "Thanks for the rescue."

"I was in the area." He presses the towel to his eye again and I catch a glimpse of strong block letters on his forearm. I want to ask to see his tattoo but I can't. It would send the wrong message. "You live far from here?"

I shake my head. I have miraculously developed a

fixation with tattoos in the last thirty seconds. "Two blocks away."

He tips his chin, studying me. The scrutiny isn't the same as the guy he ran off. There I felt hunted. Vulnerable. Like prey.

Now? Now I feel something else. Something equally unsettling but a thousand times more interesting. Something that draws me closer instead of makes me cold.

"You good to get home?"

Finally, I find my voice. "Are you my white knight in shining armor?"

He looks away and presses the towel to his eye once more.

"I'm nobody's hero," he says softly. There is something dark beneath those words. Something that should have me running in the other direction.

But I don't move. Graham would totally encourage me to go to bed with him. He claims I need someone to knock the dust off that's been gathering since the fiasco known as Robert.

I know better than to even entertain thoughts like this. I can't afford a casual hook-up like some of the blue blood sorority girls on campus. I can't afford the mistakes that can come out of them. And I damn sure can't even consider hooking up with tattooed bleeding men who apparently like to get into bar fights.

But for a moment, a brief, shining moment, I stand there and let myself get lost in the fantasy of what if. What if he took a step toward me? What if he touched his fingers to my face and whispered what he'd like to do to me? What would it feel like to grip his forearms as he slid against me, skin to skin?

Aaand I need to go home.

I'm overtired. I worked non-stop over the holiday break. That's my excuse.

It's got nothing to do with being drawn toward the big man with the dark ink on his skin and the penetrating green eyes.

The man who says he's not a hero.

"That's an odd thing to say," I say softly. I'm not going to take a single step toward him. To close the distance between us or place my hand on his chest. I'm not going to wonder what his hands would feel like on my back, his fingers tracing my spine.

Down girl.

He frowns and winces. "Never mind."

Fresh blood oozes from the cut over his eye. "You're bleeding."

"It's nothing," he says. "Happens once a week."

My throat tightens. I don't like blood. Not mine. Not anyone's.

"You should get it looked at."

His throat moves as he swallows. The ripple of skin over sinew is captivating. "I will if it doesn't stop bleeding soon."

And just like that we're at an impasse. The conversation has run its course.

"Well, thanks for...saying something." It's the most eloquent thing I can manage.

"I'm sure you could have handled it and all. I

just...I don't like...I didn't..."

His skin flushes. Beneath the shadows from the overhead light, he flushes. It's ridiculously sweet in a thousand ways.

Because I can do nothing less, I touch his upper arm. He is warm and solid and real, and for a moment, I want to be brave, or maybe foolish, and ask him his name.

But I don't. Because that's a stupid, foolish fantasy that ends with us both getting naked and me getting hurt.

And girls like me don't get the fantasy.

If we're lucky, we get the bad dream that ends in hurtful words. If we're not, we get the nightmare that maybe doesn't end.

Chapter Two

Josh

My eye is less swollen than it was last week. It hurts a hell of a lot less than it did. I can no longer feel my pulse throbbing against my bones every time I squint in the North Carolina sun.

I'll live.

I've got exactly an hour to get from my apartment off east campus to the old science building on west campus. I'll be lucky if I make it.

First day of class. Can't be late.

I should be feeling rushed and just this side of a panic attack, if the condition of the undergrads around me are any indication. But I'm not.

I'm not anything. I don't hate it here. Hate would involve feeling something. And lately, there isn't much going on with that by way of feelings.

Or maybe I've been trying to ignore the sense of alienation that hammers home the message *you don't belong here* with every beat of my heart.

I thought I'd be used to it by now. That maybe I would have found my place. But the college student remains a strange breed to me. These are not my people and this is not my space.

Half of them are wearing headphones. The other half are giggling with friends and looking around like they expect their parents to jump out from behind a bush or something. There's talk about a broken nail during a frat party from last night right behind me. Or maybe it was a broken condom. Which is actually a lot more serious but somehow, ends up discussed with the same level of intensity as the broken nail.

Really intense problems here. But I don't say anything. Because that would be rude. And I'm working on my interpersonal skills these days, or so I keep telling Eli.

I'm trying to pretend I belong here. But I don't. And I never will.

I'm wearing a long-sleeved grey t-shirt and jeans. My tattoos are hidden. I'm not wearing any camouflage, and I left my dog tags in a shoebox on the top shelf of my bedroom closet in the apartment that my GI Bill money is paying for. I won't be broke while I'm going to school. I mean, I'm not rolling in one of the many BMWs or Mercedes I see cruising around campus, but I'm not homeless and I'm not hungry so there's that.

I think they set a land speed record with my separation paperwork when we got home from that last deployment. At the time, I couldn't wait to be gone from the Army. Guess I hoped that maybe I'd feel a sense of normalcy return by now.

It hasn't.

And now, I miss it. The chaos. The waiting.

But I can't talk about those things here. If I don't open my mouth, maybe no one will figure out that I used to be a soldier.

Maybe no one will ask me what it's like to kill someone.

Funny how it hits me today of all days.

How lucky I am to be here.

How much I don't deserve it.

As I listen to the conversations and try to find some element of commonality between me and the aliens surrounding me, a single feeling slides through the noise.

I am completely exposed. I can't fucking breathe.

Today of all days, my fucking psyche has to decide to have a goddamned tantrum.

It doesn't matter that I'm fucking on one of the richest campuses in North Carolina. I'm safe. The rational part of my brain is pinging hard against the wave of panic.

It doesn't matter.

Unarmed. Unprotected. Out of uniform.

I want off campus. Away from the crowds and the noise and the problems that are so fucking trivial, I don't even know where to begin.

I round the corner to the massive quad at the center of campus, tension sliding around my ribs and squeezing my lungs until I cannot breathe. Until all I see is darkness.

I don't pass out, but it is a close thing. I double over until my vision clears.

I cannot stay here.

I need to get away. To get out.

To stop the fear from crushing the breath from my lungs.

It's the first day of my second semester at school. And I'm going to spend it in a bar.

Because drinking is cheaper than therapy.

Until it's not.

But I'll deal with that some other time. Right now, I just need to go back into the emptiness inside me.

Because the raw, ragged feelings are too much, too soon.

And I will never, ever go back to the place I once was.

I was so fucking close. So close to walking into that classroom and pretending that the last six years of my life hadn't happened. That the shitshow that was my last tour in Iraq hadn't happened. So close to pretending that I'm just another normal guy on a slightly above normal college campus.

I walk into the closest bar, which is oddly enough, a golf club near campus. I order a local beer and two shots of tequila. The tequila to take the edge off. The beer to nurse until the pain and the panic and the fear stop.

The tequila goes down easily. Too easily. I close my eyes and rest my head against the cool glass.

"You look like you're having a rough day."

The familiarity of that voice hits me all at once. If I close my eyes, I can still see her that night under the streetlight.

But she's not a memory.

I open my eyes and I am captured again by the soft gold of her eyes and the utter perfection of her smooth, dark skin.

Once, before the war, I would have flirted with her. I would have asked her for her number and if she wanted to get a drink.

Those days are nothing but a memory now. Broken by the impotent rage of combat and loss.

"Today was not a good day," is all I say instead. I hate the powerlessness in that response. The weakness.

There's a sadness in those soft golden eyes as she smiles back at me. "Can't be that bad if you're here."

She motions to the polished old money evidenced in every detail of the rich bar. There are oil canvases on the walls in heavy brass frames. Hell, the place even smells like money, or at least what I imagine money smells like. Furniture polish and leather.

We didn't have much growing up and my mom...my mom died trying to give me more.

I blink, wishing that I wasn't as hazy as I am from the alcohol. "It's not the place that's the problem."

She lifts one perfectly arched eyebrow.

It's tempting, so tempting to spill my secrets to a stranger. As if we were on a plane and I could tell her everything and she would never see me again when we landed.

But I can't take that chance here. No one knows the darkness that I struggle to hide every single day.

Every time someone thanks me for my service, I feel the need to hide what I was and what I did from the world even more.

My hand shakes as I try to take a sip of the beer. I need to get home. Out of this wide-open, dark space and away from the shame of standing in that quad as the nausea and the fear reminds me once more of what I was.

What I am.

It will never leave me.

I can feel the rush of heat across my skin. The horror mixed with the excitement. The pure, animal pleasure of it all.

It's burned into my pores, like the pounding violence of the fifty-caliber machine gun is seared into my memories.

Her touch surprises me. Jolts me out of the memories I can't escape. Her fingers are soft against the back of my hand, near my wrist.

"Hey?" I look over at her because I can do nothing less. "Are you okay?"

The shame surges inside me, smothering the thrill.

"Maybe I just wanted to have a drink." I want to flirt. To smile at her and ask her what she's doing later.

But that would be normal. And I am most assuredly not normal. Not anymore.

The words are stuck in my throat.

I look down at my beer, away from the beautiful woman with the dark skin and the light eyes standing next to me. She reminds me of things I used to want.

Maybe I'll give Eli a break and start drinking here. Maybe if I don't go to The Pint so much, I'll fight less.

Maybe if I fight less, I'll finally start to forget.

A guy can dream, right? Me and alcohol are long lost buddies.

I'm pretty sure there's a name for that. But as long as I've got my shit together, it doesn't fucking matter.

I'm not in the Army anymore. I can drink at noon if I want without anyone sending the drug and alcohol people after me.

And that's kind of terrifying.

Abby

I should walk away.

I don't need this. I need get my happy ass to class three blocks away.

But I am stuck, rooted to the pain cast in shadows at the end of the bar.

There was sadness in the way he was hunched over the bar, one hand loosely cradling a beer.

I don't know what hurt him like this. I don't know why I feel this need to care about him when I don't even know his name. There are shadows in his eyes and his mouth is set in a bleak, hard line.

And I am drawn to him. To the need to soothe his pain. To make it stop.

Maybe I'm just feeling guilty about the other night. I didn't ask him his name. I left him standing there, bleeding in the flickering shadows from the streetlight.

So instead of being smart and disciplined and focused on school, I walk up to a stranger in a bar, a man wearing a sadness beneath a dark, swollen eye.

He is so grossly out of place here it's not even funny. The men who drink here are polished and poised. There is no roughness about those men. At least not unless they've had a few too many.

Our boy here, though…There is raw power beneath the Henley stretched across his back.

And beneath that power, a darkness. Something tainted with sadness that has him chasing it away with beer before ten a.m.

I can see him visibly trying to relax. He's breathing slow and deep. I recognize the gesture. I've done it often enough myself.

I don't hate men. I haven't even sworn off dating. But I'm tender from my ex's hateful words the last time I saw him. I'm wary.

Even as I push my friends toward their own happiness, I hold back.

Because it hurts to love the wrong man.

He looks over at me and I can feel the pull of that darkness. That familiar desire is back. The need to fix things. Not things. People.

I can't do this again. Not with him. Not with anyone. I need a nice, normal, well-adjusted guy. Not someone with shadows beneath his eyes who starts drinking before the sun reaches its peak in the sky.

But I don't move. Don't do the smart thing and leave him sitting there.

I lean on the bar next to him. Side by side. Cradle my head in my hand and just wait. Casual. Pretending my lungs aren't too tight and my body isn't too aware of the size and strength in this man.

He lifts the glass to his lips and just like last Friday, I am mesmerized by the movement in his throat. Who knew something as mundane as swallowing could be so captivating?

I am not going to think about pressing my lips to the pulse in his throat. Or running my fingers down that same spot.

"Want to talk about it?" How's that for witty? I need Flirting for Dummies or something.

There is a scab over his right eye. "Are you my fairy god-therapist?"

I shrug. "Nah. Just thought I'd offer. You know, return the favor from the other night."

His lips are flat and tight. "I run off a dude hassling you, and now you get to listen to me solve all the world's problems?"

"Maybe not the world. How about just yours?" He's prickly but I'm not afraid of him. There is something about him that feels...not safe. That's the wrong word. No, never that. But something that makes the risk...worth it. "I'm a pretty good listener."

He turns back to his drink and tosses back the remains. "It's complicated."

"Always is."

He rests his forehead against the empty glass and looks so broken and sad, it cracks the ice around my heart just a little bit.

I reach out. Hesitant. More afraid of his reaction than my own. My fingers brush against his shoulder before coming to rest on his upper arm. "Hey."

It's a long moment before he looks at me.

I immediately remove my hand from his arm. There is a coldness in his eyes. A threat of violence for invading his space.

Message received.

Graham walks in at that moment, rescuing both of us from my awkward attempt at comfort.

My hand is shaking from the encounter when I reach for my check from him.

"You working tonight?" Graham asks.

"You know it." I shoot him a look, willing him to leave me alone.

Graham pins me with a lifted eyebrow, and I shake my head slightly. Please don't say anything.

But not our Graham. My best friend leans against the bar and taps the polished mahogany in front of Mr. Tall, Dark and Psychotic. "So our girl Fergalicious here is recently single, having had her heart stomped on by a bastard of an ex who I am obligated to hate for the rest of our natural lives. She's studying public policy and has a natural talent for upside-down pineapple cake that really should be listed on her resumé."

There is curiosity now in those dark green eyes. Gone is the cold threat of violence. Like it was never there.

But it's not something I can forget so easily.

Because I know what I saw. I know where the bruise over his eye came from. A man like this…I know this kind of violence. This kind of rapid change in temper and mood.

And that's my cue to get the hell away from him.

I look at the massive oak clock over the bar and fight the urge to stab Graham. He means well but damn it, just because he's started dating Mr. Right doesn't mean he gets to find my happily ever after for me. "Yeah. Anyway. I'll see you tonight, Graham."

Graham, of course, takes that opportunity to sneak away. Leaving me alone again with…him.

"Wait; you work here?"

So, of course, I'm standing here, answering the question he asked, and wondering about the ones he doesn't. "Is that bad?" I ask cautiously.

"No. Just surprising." His voice is warmer now, his words thick.

"Why?"

"I figured everyone at this school is…not the kind of people that have to work their way through college."

In my head, I smile and pat his cheek in a slightly flirty and not quite condescending way.

In reality, I stand there, thinking of all the ways I

could respond. "Well, that's what you get for stereotyping me," I say with a gentle smile. "Though I've never been mistaken for wealthy. I have been asked if I wanted to pay for something with cash or food stamps."

He looks down my body, then back up. I can't help but feel like I just went through some kind of inspection. I'm not even sure if I've passed or not. "That's pretty fucked up."

"You've never been stereotyped?"

He stiffens. It's subtle, but there in the slight flare of his nostrils, the tightness in his back. He tries to play it off but I've been watching people for far too long. "People think I'm wealthy because I drink here."

It's a lie. One I might not have caught if I hadn't been paying attention.

"I've never seen you here before."

"It's my first time."

And just like that, I am completely confused by the man sitting in front of me.

He is a puzzle. One for someone else to solve.

I walk away before I do something infinitely stupid.

Like ask him his name.

Chapter Three

Josh

I suppose there are worse ways to die. My head feels like the inside of a tunnel with a fifty cal going off. The reverberations are echoing inside my skull with every beat of my pulse, and I'm reasonably certain I'm going to die if I don't get some coffee and a hell of a lot more Motrin than I've currently got in my system. Which, at the moment, is zero.

And as much as I feel like the inside of a bucket of shit, I've definitely had worse hangovers in my life.

If I'm honest with myself, I'm really stalling.

I don't want to go back on campus. I don't want to risk another episode like the other day.

And I don't want to go to the particular class I've got today. Not at fucking all. I'm not really sure why I need this specific class and I'm half tempted to bring a flask just in case things get a little froggy.

Because I don't need an academic discussion of violence. Not when I've been up close and personal with the real thing.

I tried to argue with my advisor about it, but Professor Blake wasn't really interested in all the perfectly valid reasons why I did not need to take this class.

I manage to make it to the campus coffee shop, appropriately named The Grind, at that magical thirty-second interlude where the line isn't wrapped around the library. A double shot of espresso ought to get me through the morning. At least I hope it will. It's not as potent as Green Bean from back in Kuwait, but it'll do. I suppose I can always chew some espresso beans if I get really antsy. Caffeine calms me down the way it amps other people up.

Guess I'm kind of strange like that.

I almost grab a donut but decide against it. Everything is too sweet for me. You'd think after being home for as long as I have, I'd be back to normal by now.

Some things are just damn hard to get used to.

I walk through campus toward the anthropology building. I don't say hi to the people I pass. I'm only a few years older than most of them but there is no common ground between us. No way to meet in the middle.

It's like that guy from the bar last week. He thinks violence is never the answer.

Our understanding of how the world works is one hundred percent mutually exclusive.

I manage to find my class and spoiler alert, I'm early. And by early I mean on time.

It's a character flaw. I can't not be early to any appointment. Guess it was driven into my DNA during basic training and I've never really bothered to change the habit since I left the Army. Not only did you have to be ten minutes prior to anything, but you also had to be ten minutes prior to the first sergeant's ten minutes prior. I remember being actively shocked when people strolled into my class ten minutes late. It was like a physical reaction.

I imagined my first sergeant going up one side of them and down the other.

And then I remember I'm not in Kansas anymore. There are no first sergeants here. I'm slowly coming to the conclusion that this is their reality. It's not mine and it never will be. I'll never be the guy who rides the bus across campus and flirts with the cute chick in Chemistry.

But my classmates? They never give it another thought and that's not a bad thing. Man, one dude with an AR-15 and a superiority complex could wreck this place.

But it'll never happen here. This isn't the kind of place those things happen. Those things only happen at "other places" where the students aren't all rich kids.

And I try, I really try not to stare in disbelief at the First World problems I'm not used to hearing.

Wouldn't it be a perfect introduction to the class for me to lose my shit on some pretentious asshole for bitching about his parking spot or how Whole Foods was out of his favorite quinoa?

I take another sip of coffee, trying to keep myself amused as I step into the classroom.

It's a super human effort not to stop, stunned and rooted to the spot. Holy shit, it's her.

I cannot look away. Across the distance and the noise, she is a beacon. A center of calm in the frenetic motion of the classroom.

The girl from the bar. Alone, off to one side. Like the rest of the class doesn't know what to do with her because her skin is darker than theirs. Or maybe Daddy doesn't have the right pedigree.

If she notices the way her classmates move around her like she's not there, she's playing it cool. Texting someone.

I imagine it's very alienating.

I know all about that.

I swallow and summon up the courage I need to approach her. 'Cause it's a whole new ball game talking to a girl when I haven't been drinking.

Especially one as stunning as she is.

"Mind if I join you?"

She looks up sharply, her eyes wide, as though she's completely surprised by my question. Which I suppose says enough about the quality of interactions on campus.

I have the distinct impression that she sees me, the real me. Not the hunched-over-the-bar-and-one-sad-story-away-from-eating-a-fucking-bullet-for-breakfast me. No, not that me. The me beneath the scars and the ink and the scruff.

"Sure." She's watching me carefully. I'm definitely being inspected. For what failings, I'm not sure.

I sit. Not right next to her, because that would be

kind of strange in a room that has as many empty seats as it does. I leave a single seat between us and try to do the mindless prep for class rituals my classmates appear to be doing.

I'm getting ready to summon up the courage to ask her what her name is when I get a second unpleasant surprise. Two in one week. Well, I only need one more for the shit show trifecta to be complete.

Parker Hauser breezes into class like a force of nature. It's a certain way that women like her carry themselves around here but Parker, Parker has perfected it and it's annoying as fuck. She was in one of my classes last semester and she annoyed me to no end talking about personal responsibility and rational choice theory. Before I remembered that I was a founding member of the fucking nuts club, I'd tried to engage with her arguments. Now? Now if she starts in on her rational choice theory bullshit, I might just completely lose my shit. Again.

"Oh great," I mumble.

"Friend of yours?" I am very much drawn to the sound of her voice. I wish we were alone. So I could do something daring and bold. Like talk to her while being cold sober.

"Not really." The anxiety catches in my throat, squeezing tight. I take another sip of my coffee and watch my cellmates—I mean classmates—filter in, trying not to feel awkward and weird that I don't know what to say to the girl I'm not quite sitting next to.

Maybe if I had a drink or two in me, I'd finally find something witty to say. Maybe I'd be able to ask her why she was in this particular class without choking on the nervousness. Maybe I'd finally feel something around a girl.

Except I haven't felt that kind of excitement in a long, long time. And it's not likely to change any time soon.

And holy hell, I am not confronting that unpleasant memory today. I mean, what in the world is wrong with this week? It's like my psyche is deliberately fucking with me.

And honestly, I don't need any damn help in that department.

The professor walks in. I suppose it's strange that I'm relieved and disappointed all at once.

It's actually a good thing he showed up. Because a thought had taken hold – this idea that maybe, I could actually have a conversation that didn't involve alcohol. That maybe I could flirt and pretend that I'm just another guy in the dating pool.

I'm meant to be alone. If I wasn't sure about that before the war, I damn sure am now.

Professor Quinn finally starts class, ending any chance I have to talk to her.

Which means she'll be safe.

At least from me.

Abby

I am struck silent the moment he walks into the classroom.

Even more so when he scans the room briefly then his gaze settles on me. Only me. I am poignantly aware of my skin fitting too tightly over my bones.

I can't explain my reaction to seeing him here, in my space. There is a sense of anticipation, a warmth flowing through me.

If I really investigate what I am feeling, it is…that anticipation just before hope turns into something else. There is no reason why I should react this way to a man I've spoken to exactly twice.

He seems darker here. More threatening and out of place. Here I can clearly see the hard lines of his face beneath the stubble. The penetrating green of his eyes is focused one hundred percent on me.

He is still as the world moves around him. The motionless energy of a predator watching his prey.

Which would be me.

And I am not afraid.

No, it's definitely not fear coursing through my veins at the moment.

It's something decidedly different when he approaches and asks if he can sit next to me.

Just like that, I am no longer alone on the edge of the classroom.

I am used to sitting by myself. I barely even notice it anymore.

In that single span of time when the space close to me goes from empty to filled, something shifts inside me.

I release a hard breath. It should not be a big deal that maybe a guy wants to actually talk to me. It shouldn't be and yet, it is.

Maybe Graham is right and I do need to knock the dust off.

For once I am not alone and I have no idea what to do with that feeling. Maybe I can assume risk this once and allow myself the pleasure of a fantasy daydream.

If I close my eyes, I can let myself imagine his fingers on my neck. A simple gesture that is both erotic and comforting all at once.

Something no lover has ever done to me publicly.

Something I need to give myself permission to want. To let myself crave. Today, I want to imagine his fingers on my skin. His breath mingling with mine, the woodsy taste of scotch on his tongue.

The fantasy comes to a screeching halt. Wow, my life is a real beacon of hope for strong women everywhere. The only guy who seems to get me hot and bothered was drinking before noon yesterday.

I want to know his name. I've decided that already. I should text Graham and ask him if he knows it. But that would clue Graham in that I was interested, and while I love Graham like a brother, he has far too much invested in my love life or lack thereof. He'd give the guy my number, home address, and blood type if he thought it would get me laid.

I might make jokes about it, but I'm not that open when it comes to sex. It's not that I'm morally opposed to it. But it hasn't been exactly…earth shattering for me. Robert was…more concerned with his own pleasure than mine.

And wow, do I need to think about something else. Something other than the man next to me with the haunted eyes and thick, blunt fingers that are currently toying with a pencil.

Down, girl.

I'm better than this. I'm not boy crazy. I don't let myself get distracted from why I'm here and guys definitely fall into the distraction category these days. I know who I am and what I want in life. And while the fantasy of having a guy stroke my neck and whisper things to make me laugh might be appealing, it's nothing more than a fantasy for girls like me in a place like this.

Fantasies are safe.

Fantasies don't ruin your life and crush your soul and try to change who you are. They don't pretend to love you.

And in my fantasies is where he'll stay. In the dark and the shadows, where I can take out the idea of him and play with it for a little while, then put it safely away where it can wait until next time.

Because fantasies can't hurt you.

And as interested as I am in the man who did such a simple thing by sitting next to me, I am far too cynical to pretend that this is anything more than it is—a kind gesture.

Nothing more.

Chapter Four

Josh

I really should say something. Introduce myself. It feels really stalker-esque to think of her as her.

And when class doesn't start because the projector isn't working, I realize I have another opportunity to not be a fucking coward and actually talk to her.

I'm curious. Despite all my good intentions of keeping my distance, I want to know what on earth compelled her to approach me yesterday at the bar. I want to know what inspired her to stand and fight instead of try to downplay the situation on the street outside The Pint last week.

I worked with a female soldier back in my unit. She wasn't officially assigned to us, which was why she was the only one around. She was badass on a weapons system but she never would have stood her ground like the girl next to me did the other night. She always traded cheap shots with the NCOs until they stopped hassling her. Deflection and de-escalation through dick jokes.

But the confrontation isn't what has me intrigued. At least not completely.

I want to know why she approached me. Why she talked to me at the bar. Why she pretended to care.

Women don't do that. And women who work in bars damn sure don't do that. Not if they're smart.

I know what she said. But people never tell the truth about stuff like that. They always have ulterior motives.

Funny, I can't figure out what hers might be. I'm usually better at reading people but she's got me stumped.

There's something about her that draws my attention. Maybe it's the tight curls that frame her face, drifting around her neck. Maybe it's the way she observed the entire room with her golden eyes that give you the impression she doesn't miss the smallest detail.

I steal a glance over at her, trying to be smooth and not completely fucking obvious.

She is focused on her paper, her right hand furiously scratching notes out in scrawling, neat penmanship. But her left hand is resting at the base of her throat. Her fingers sliding gently over her smooth skin, almost absently. Almost as though she wasn't paying attention to the lecture but instead, lost in a fantasy.

For a moment, I'm enthralled by the movement. The slide of a single finger over soft, soft skin. The feel of your lover's pulse racing beneath your caress. The power of a touch that says you are mine.

I haven't been touched like that in a long, long

time.

I look away, seized by a sense of loss almost as powerful as the panic from yesterday.

I have to admit, I'm mildly relieved when Professor Quinn pulls up PowerPoint for his lecture.

Death by PowerPoint even in college. But sometimes, it's the familiar that offers comfort.

Except that now I'm paying for the privilege of being lulled to sleep by slides.

Quinn is a short, skinny guy who looks like a fifty-year-old version of the aging hipster. Maybe he's the original hipster. With his thick glasses and greying goatee, he looks like what I imagine Colonel Sanders of the KFC variety would look like as a college professor.

He finally starts his lecture. There's no good morning. No here's what we're going to talk about today. No lesson objectives.

Guess I'm not in Kansas anymore. An Army slide would have been carefully scripted with lesson objectives, key concepts and a course guide.

Looks like I'm supposed to think for myself here, too.

Which is kind of terrifying in a lot of ways.

"So let's talk about ISIS today. From your readings, you see they're in the news this week because of their beheading of another American citizen. What do you think motivates these people to do such a horrific act?"

From the front left, a hand shoots up into the air. Spoiler alert, it's Parker. Here we go. She's what we call a spring butt in the Army. The first person to raise their hand and always has something they think is brilliant to say.

Her voice is pitch perfect in a super-annoying Elle Woods kind of way. Except that she doesn't have the dorky charm of Elle Woods. And no, I'm not embarrassed for having watched Legally Blonde on my last deployment.

Parker is confident in a way that suggests prep school and a mother with a ruler and a strong look of disappointment if she so much as looked at something the wrong way or dared to have her own opinion about anything.

"They're completely insane," she says.

I look down at my paper. I do not want to talk about this shit today. Or ever, for that matter. This class is a massive fucking mistake. It needs a fucking trigger warning.

My advisor and I are going to have a serious discussion about why she thinks this class is necessary for my degree. I want to do Homeland Security consulting. I know more than enough about violence and conflict management.

I wonder when the drop deadline is. Or if I can change majors. Maybe I can bribe my advisor to let me take something else. I'll claim psychological distress or something.

But then they might ask for a mental health evaluation and god forbid should the veteran have mental health issues. And I'm most certainly not doing one of those. They might discover my other problem.

Parker continues. "They're using horrific violence as shock value, nothing more. If they were better integrated in society, they wouldn't have run off to join this band of murdering psychopaths."

She's so wrong it's not even funny. Guess a lack of cultural understanding isn't unique to the Army.

"Mr. Douglas, you disagree."

Fuck.

I look up to find the entire class has turned around, waiting for my answer.

I grind my teeth, wondering how the hell I managed to draw attention to myself.

Guess it's my fucking super power.

I wonder what they'd do if I ran screaming from the room, yelling for everyone to take cover. It's how I feel right now. Like they're waiting for me to grow a second head.

But those are my issues, not theirs; because none of them know I'm a soldier. It's all in my head. Most of them probably have no idea that I should have a blazing neon sign over my head that says Warning: Angry Veteran. May snap if provoked.

The only war they know about is the one they see on TV. Or the one that could happen if Starbucks runs out of their favorite espresso.

"They're not psychopaths." I keep my voice calm and level and speak extra slowly. I need to keep my emotion out of this entire exchange and that is getting more and more difficult by the moment. "Just because someone is willing to engage in violence does not make them crazy."

Parker launches into her defense before I barely finish talking.

"No, I'm not willing to acknowledge that. Studies have consistently demonstrated that people who engage in this level of violence are severely mentally disturbed."

I smile at her and it is as cold and dead as I feel inside. She has no idea what life outside the smooth stone walls of this campus and her gated community is like.

"So explain all of human history," I say. "We used to gather in the town square for stoning as Saturday night entertainment."

I made that up. I think. But she's wrong.

She's fucking wrong.

The girl next to me shakes her head and lifts her hand. "Whether or not members of ISIS are mentally ill is irrelevant, isn't it? I mean, we're not going to assess their mental health before we launch drones at them."

Professor Quinn motions to her, not dismissing her remarks like he's done to mine.

She is rapidly becoming my obsession. "Go further with that, Ms. Hilliard. What do you mean?"

Hilliard.

At least now I have her name.

Abby

I have a rule about talking in class. If I wouldn't say it to the whole room, I don't say anything. And now, I'm diving into a conversation that is incredibly uncomfortable. Well, that's what I get for opening my mouth in class.

Here goes nothing.

"We're engaged in a drone war across half the Middle East and those are the countries we publicly know about. We know ISIS are cutting people's heads off. We're not going to capture them and put them on trial; we're going to bomb them. So what does it matter why they're doing what they're doing?" I shift in my seat so I can see Mr. Douglas—because thanks to Professor Quinn I actually know his name now—and Parker at the same time.

I am shocked by the transformation in him. Before where he'd been dark and brooding, he's...different now. Something energized. Something...else. The veins in his neck are standing out and the muscles are visibly pulsing. He looks worse—if that is actually possible—than he did at the bar yesterday.

And just like yesterday, I have a striking urge to ask him if he's okay.

Instead, Parker draws my attention from him. "I have to agree with Abby. I don't think it matters. But I think they're cray."

I roll my eyes but he speaks up.

"I think calling them 'cray'"—and he practically

sneers the word—"discounts what they're doing and what they're capable of."

Professor Quinn tips his chin at him, either completely unaware of the tension radiating off him or ignoring it. I'm not sure which one would actually be better. "And what are they doing, Mr. Douglas?"

"They're building a movement," Douglas says. "These people are not psychopaths. They're deeply motivated believers in what they're doing."

"Ha, so it is religious," Parker says suddenly.

Douglas frowns, as though the point were never up for debate. "I don't think there's any doubt in that."

"And we know that religious brains have less functioning in the areas that promote rational thought. They're more emotional, less reasonable. They are actually quite different from normal people," she says.

He is shaking his head again. "That's fundamentally the wrong way to look at this. Just because you can't imagine belonging to something else so strongly that you'd die for it doesn't mean that people who do are mentally ill."

Well, this just took a turn for the worse. And by worse I mean personal.

My hands are slick with sweat.

Violence and mental illness and religion are not things I want to dig up and explore in some sanitized classroom. They're not theoretical abstractions in my world.

There's silence in the classroom now and it

spreads like an eighth-grade rumor.

Professor Quinn holds up his hands, silencing the debate. "This is fundamentally the problem with all extremist movements," he says. For a little man, he's got a strong voice. Reminds me of my Uncle Richie, who was the quintessential child of the '60s, who refused to shave his white beard or his grey ponytail long after that glorious decade of debauchery was over.

The disparity between Professor Quinn's voice and his body isn't easy to overcome, but he's put his voice to good use by drawing all of our attention to him.

"Anything that can motivate individuals to sacrifice themselves for the group is toying with a dangerous ideology," Parker says. "It's brainwashing."

Everyone turns as Mr. Douglas cuts Parker off. "Show me the evidence where it's brainwashing."

There's violence radiating off him right now. Stress is a palpable thing. I want to interject, to stop this because I can see so clearly where this whole thing is going and it's not going to be good.

Quinn has a reputation. He likes to start massive arguments in his class, then when things get out of control, he's likely to throw your happy ass out of class with a quickness.

"I'm sorry," Parker says and her voice is dripping with condescension. "But that's exactly the problem. These groups trigger something in people that make them lose their sense of self. It's completely irrational." She shifts back toward Professor Quinn. "It's like when people were protesting us leaving Iraq. It was stupid to leave soldiers there. We had no business invading, and leaving was the most rational thing this administration could have done. No boots on the ground is smart."

Douglas leans forward, his eyes dark and flashing. Professor Quinn has shifted, folding his arms over his chest. Watching. Waiting.

"We damn sure do have boots on the ground."

Parker makes a noise. "We don't have any soldiers in Iraq anymore." There's casual arrogance in her answer, and it grates on my nerves even though it's directed at Douglas for once and not at me.

"Really? Check your news, there, princess. We've got almost five thousand troops on the ground and more on the way." I hope Professor Quinn can't see his fists bunched in his lap. "We continue to be and have never stopped being at war," he says quietly. "And violence is the only way to deal with some people."

"Violence is never the solution to problems," Parker says. "We need to figure out what ISIS is really after and negotiate."

He tenses then. His fists are tight beneath his desk, his knuckles white against his skin. "They have told us what they are after. Your refusal to believe them is your problem, not theirs."

"That's not true," Parker said. "These people only want jobs and normal lives like the rest of us."

"That's a stupid and naïve way to look at the

world," he says and his tone is ugly and hard.

I can't look away from the tension radiating off him. This is not anger at a debate gone wrong.

This is personal.

And I have a burning need to know why.

Chapter Five

Josh

Let's not devolve into personal attacks," Quinn finally interrupts.

I'm breathing hard now. My fists are tight in my lap. I can't stop. I want to shut my mouth but everything is spinning too fast, too far out of control. I need to get out. Get away. I can't do this. My advisor was wrong. So fucking wrong. I can't do this.

Ms. Hilliard breaks through the vibrating anger in my brain. "I thought we were going to be able to discuss things? Isn't that what college is all about?"

She draws Quinn's attention away from me, and for a moment, I sit there and just try to breathe. To yank my temper and my emotions back under control.

I am falling. Again. Into the rage and the hate and the anger.

"He's clearly personally involved in this," Parker says, and there is a barely concealed sneer in her words.

"So what if he is?" My protector shakes her head. Slow and smooth and steady. She's amazing. "I don't think we should automatically discount his argument just because it doesn't mesh with what we've been taught. He's arguing for a position that's pretty foreign from the homogenous environment that we usually find ourselves in."

I narrow my eyes and wish I didn't understand what she'd just said, but my brain has been rewired since I started school here. Words like "homogenous" and "heterogeneity" are now part of my vocabulary and I can't undo that. We couldn't just say "similarity within groups". Oh no, we have to make up big words to show how intellectually superior we are.

I rub my hand over my face, trying to yank my thoughts back from the edge of the abyss. I ball my hands up in my lap and struggle to drag my emotions under control and pray to a God that I don't believe in that the conversation will move beyond the current impasse.

But oh no, Parker just has to keep going.

"Look, I appreciate diversity of opinions, but let's be honest. Arguing that violence is the solution to any problem isn't appropriate in academia. The only people who support violence are those who get hard ons from playing first person shooter games."

She stabs me then, right in the soft spot, and there is no way she did it on purpose. But it still hurts.

I'm about to pipe off with something deeply inappropriate but at the last minute, I yank myself back and refocus. Breathing. One. Two. Three.

My savior next to me continues on the offense. "You're failing to attack the argument on its merit and only attacking it based on the fact that you don't like where it takes us."

Professor Quinn, apparently, has decided to pull his man card and control his class. And by that I mean me.

"I think we've gotten as much out of this argument as we can. There's value in having these differing opinions but if we shout each other down, are we really listening to each other or just waiting for our own biases to be confirmed?"

Abby

The sunlight hurts my eyes. It was cloudy and overcast before class started, the sky swollen and threatening rain. Now, the clouds have burned away, leaving the sky brilliant and blue.

I slide my sunglasses on and feel him step into the light with me. "That went well," he says mildly.

He sounds far too calm for what just happened. I saw the tension in his body during that debate. I saw his hands fisted in his lap.

He was not calm. So why the hell is he acting like they just argued about the best flavor of coffee?

"What...what was that?" I say. Because I can't help myself.

There's a tiny crease at the corner of his mouth

that I've never noticed before. Just the tiniest little line that draws my attention to his ridiculously full bottom lip. It's actually the only thing soft on him.

At least, as far as I'm aware of. And wow, talk about a stunning mental detour.

"A purely academic debate about violence," he says mildly.

"You were a little more wound up." I honestly can't say why I'm out here, talking to him. I need to go. To get away from the strength and power in those hands. "And now you're acting all calm, cool, and collected. What gives?"

He looks at me sharply and I feel pinned to the spot. Like I've been cornered by a caged mountain lion and I'm wearing a steak jumpsuit. "You really want to know?"

Whenever anyone asks a question like that, it's generally a good idea to answer no and get the hell out of Dodge.

But, of course, I stay right there. I fold my arms over my chest. "Yeah. I do."

He stiffens a little. "It's...you. You and Parker and all these professors. You sit around and wax poetic about violence and starvation and inequality while sitting on one of the wealthiest college campuses in the South. Completely safe. No risk. And then people like Parker judge people like me who have to make those decisions."

"And live with the consequences," I whisper.

He hesitates. His mouth opens, then snaps closed. Like my answer surprises him as much as it does me.

"Yeah."

He's watching me. I want to step closer to him but I can't. I won't.

Because I'm not blind to the darkness in Mr. Douglas. It's there, just below the surface. Like a pot of water just before it boils.

The tension is back, now. A slow burning anger I should be getting as far away from as I possibly can.

"What?" I finally ask, needing something to break the spell between us.

"Why do you care why I got angry in class? You don't even know my name."

I narrow my eyes at him and open my mouth, then snap it closed, mirroring his earlier action. I didn't expect the question and I have no idea how to answer.

Because in reality, I don't have an answer for why I'm standing here at the moment.

Damn it.

My brain finally latches on to the first thing I come up with.

"Wookie life debt. Payback for you helping me the other night."

I try to leave then. Hoping that he'll let me go and put all my curiosity away. For good.

"Hey." His voice tugs at me to stop.

I won't look at him now. Because I'm ashamed of what he'll see if he looks into my eyes.

And I can't stand the thought of him seeing the needful loneliness that has become my constant companion since Robert ripped my heart out and left it bleeding on the cobblestone sidewalk.

"What's your name?" His voice is low and quiet. Steady now. Almost calm.

I turn, unable to avoid looking at him now.

It dawns on me that no, I don't know his name.

I stand there for a moment, hesitant. The last time this happened, I fell too far, too fast.

This time will be different. Because I'm not going to make the same mistake twice.

It's like standing too close to an electrical current.

The simplicity of the question is deceptively benign.

I'm drawn to him in a way that is unhealthy and dangerous. He's already consuming my thoughts, drawing my attention away from the matter at hand and luring me down a dark corridor where only dark thoughts and whispered need twist together.

I hold up one hand, needing to break the spell or whatever is going on between us. My hand collides with his chest, and I am flush against the stark reminder of this man's strength and power and capability to do violence.

Before the rational part of my brain kicks in, I brush my fingertips gently over the bruised and damaged skin above his eye.

He goes still beneath my touch. That full bottom lip opens a little. A tiny space, but I can feel the heat of his breath on my wrist.

His eyes are locked on mine. I'm trapped, unable

to move. I'm not sure I want to. I'm furious for him but I'm frozen, burning where my fingers touch his skin.

I cannot move. Cannot look away.

"I'm Josh," he whispers. An answer to an unasked question.

I swallow the sudden lump blocking my throat. "Abby."

"Abby." He repeats my name and it sounds something like a prayer, whispered in reverence and awe.

I lower my hand then but he catches it. His palm is rough and big, surrounding mine. "It's nice to meet you, Abby," he says softly.

And I say nothing. Because in his eyes I see a hint of something I am longing for.

And it is something that terrifies me.

Chapter Six

Josh

I have to stop thinking about her. I have to put her out of my mind and crawl back into the dead space where I've been living since I came home from the war.

It really sucks when you're trying to crawl into a bottle because you need to stop thinking about things and can't summon the energy to get blasted. I'm tired of listening to the voice in my head, and I'm hoping to drown that little fucker.

It keeps whispering that I'll fuck up. That I'll say the wrong thing and everyone can look at me and see the blood and the gore and the twisted parody of humanity that I'm pretending to be. All the memories are circling tonight because I've met her. Abby.

Making me want to pretend I'm not a fucking monster. Making me want to forget everything that has come before, that's made me into the half man I am today. All of it. Burning my skin again, searing my nose with the smell of blood and fire and the wild thrilling shame of it.

I head to The Pint, because I don't keep alcohol

in my apartment. That would make it too easy to sit in the dark and drink by myself. Drinking is only a problem when you hide it, right?

I'm not hiding it. No, I'm about to get fucked up in public at the only place that feels even remotely like somewhere I fit. Maybe I should ask Eli for a job. I spend enough time here.

"Ah fuck." My BFF Caleb is sitting at the bar, shooting the shit with Eli. And by BFF, I mean a guy I wouldn't piss on if he was on fire. The last thing I want is to listen to him chest-beating about how much action he saw downrange. How the hell can Eli tolerate that guy?

I met him here a few months back with a couple of the other vets here on campus. He's a former West Point officer, which—unfortunately—should tell you something right there. Ninety percent of the kids who come out of West Point are normal, well-adjusted adults. Like Eli. Except that Eli was the kid leading the insurgency at West Point. Not Caleb.

No, he's one of the ones who gets high on power and authority and forgets that there are people executing the orders he gives.

God but I hate officers like Caleb. Spineless fucks who talk about how awesome it was at war, blowing shit up. Like he gets off on the very thought of it.

And what's nuts is that Caleb thinks we're actually friends.

And there's a happy mental image that I'm about to try and drown with some alcohol. I'm not in the mood to listen to Caleb on a good day, but because I need a drink, I walk up to the bar and mumble something vaguely polite and order a beer.

Praise Jesus, Caleb ducks away to the latrine.

"You going to behave tonight?" Eli asks, sliding a beer in front of me.

"I shall give it my best effort," I say with a grin that's about as genuine as I'm feeling right now.

He glares at me in the way that reminds me of my old first sergeant. "Think of the children. Or if nothing else, think of me having to order new bar stools if you break another one."

Eli is a study in contradictions. He runs a bar—correction: a craft brewery—but I'm pretty sure he's got a graduate degree from the business school here, which is one of the top business schools in the country. West Point grads tend to be clean-cut and on the tight side of uptight but he's also sporting full sleeves of tattoos on both arms and a beard that puts the members of the local chapter of Hell's Angels to shame.

I snort and take a long pull off the beer. It's the perfect balm to a really odd start to the semester.

Eli changes the channel on the TV over the bar.

The newscaster's face is polished and tight with too much plastic surgery. There's a false somberness as he reports the latest news from the war.

FOB overrun within five hours. Seven coalition forces killed in the heavy fighting over three days in the mountains near the Pakistan border.

"Change the fucking channel." I don't beg. I can't

go that far. But I can't watch this. Not tonight.

"Hang on."

I don't know Eli's story but I know he doesn't turn the war off. Doesn't avoid it like I do. He watches the news incessantly.

But then Caleb returns.

"Hey, dude. How's the first week of classes going?"

See? He thinks we're friends. And when he's not being a deliberate tool, I have to be polite. Because he's one of Eli's stray veterans he keeps rounding up from the local area. And we're supposed to stick together or some shit.

"Surviving. You?" I can be polite.

"Pretty good. I'm doing an independent study with the head of the law department." He shifts his attention to the news from Afghanistan. "Fuck man, I wish I was there right now. They wouldn't have taken the base if I'd been in command." He takes another pull from his beer. "We'd blow those motherfuckers to Kingdom Come. Let God sort 'em out."

"I'm sure you would." I try, I really try to keep the sarcasm to a minimum.

I don't really succeed.

"What. You know what it's like, man. The fucking charge you get when you blow one of those fuckers away."

I take a long pull off my beer. I do know. And I do not want to fucking talk about it. "You know the Green Zone wasn't exactly fucking Fallujah, right?"

Eli sets another beer in front of me. "Not tonight, Josh."

"We got bombed. Every day," Caleb says mildly.

I shrug. "Sure there were a few attacks. But for the most part, it was goddamned Disney World."

"Disney World doesn't have incoming mortar fires, now does it?"

I smile coldly. "From six miles away. Dude, the closest thing to tragedy at the Green Zone was the Olympic swimming pool running out of chlorine tablets."

"What the hell is your problem?" Caleb rounds on me. "I don't have enough PTSD or something?"

I down the rest of my beer. "You know, I came in here to grab a beer, not listen to some prima donna officer bitch jack off to bullshit war stories."

"Oh, come on. You know you liked it. Everyone fucking likes blowing shit up."

I did like it. And that's ninety percent of the fucking problem.

I've never felt so alone when surrounded by so many people.

I push away from the bar. "I gotta go." I slap money on the counter. "You should really clean the place up," I say to Eli. "Keep enough guys around who are as full of shit as this guy, real vets will start to stay away."

I just need some space. Some air. Some fucking perspective on why I can't ever seem to control my fucking temper.

I am at one of the top schools in the country. I

am surrounded by expensive cars and old money and I have never felt more out of place in my life. And yes, that includes when I was in Iraq.

I look down at my hands as I step outside into the cool North Carolina night, lean against the damp brick wall and try to catch my breath.

All I can see is the blood beneath my nails. The red painting my skin again. The burning shame as the memory of the excitement mixes with the pure horror of what I've done.

I can't see the stars, but the moon is bright enough that it penetrates the illumination from the streetlights.

I start walking. Down the silent, dark street illuminated by flickering overhead lamps.

The voice in my head is silent now. Leaving me alone in the darkness as I walk toward my tiny loft.

Except that I don't end up at my place.

I end up in the glittering, polished foyer of the Baywater. I have no business here. I shouldn't have come.

But I'm here now, standing in the middle of so much wealth and class I feel like I am a speck of dirt dragged in from the outside on the bottom of someone's five hundred-dollar shoes.

I'm tainting this place with my very presence. And still, I cannot leave.

There is a dinner party in one of the rooms. Which has its own name, apparently: The Winston Bonaparte room. I watch them for a while, trying to figure out what to say, what to do, why I'm here.

It is a long moment before I see her.

Abby.

She doesn't notice me. I can stand there, silently, and just watch her move. There is a fluidity in how she moves with an easy grace and class that I will never have. She smiles at a man wearing an expensive suit and tie. He's clean shaven, and I'd be willing to bet he doesn't have any tattoos or scars from a war he never even thought about fighting in.

I need to go before Abby notices me. I don't belong here.

Not like she does.

But if I'm honest with myself, she is the reason I am here. She's a beacon in the darkness, drawing me closer to something I have given up wanting.

She stops short when she sees me.

There is no smile in her eyes. No warmth. I don't have the words to explain to her why I'm here.

But as much as I can't explain why I'm here, I also can't walk away. I have no business here. I have no business talking to her.

I can't protect her from me. I can't even protect myself.

But I cannot walk away.

Abby

My shift has been extra magical tonight, and by extra magical I mean slammed busy. Which is fine.

I'm one of those weird people who doesn't actually know how to sit still. I'm always moving. I thrive on being busy, which is strange considering I'm in the South and things tend to move a bit slower around here.

I'm waiting on a table of the dean of the business school and his polished and manicured guest. The woman on the guest's arm looks like she could be his daughter but I learned early on not to make assumptions about those sorts of things here. I make small talk and smile, not really hearing what the dean or his guest are saying.

The moment I see Josh, though, everything else falls away. Their noise, their needs. Everything I am is focused on Josh.

He is darkness and shadows near the edge of the dim light. He doesn't even pretend he's not watching me. It does something to my insides as I meet his eyes and refuse to look away.

In the shadows, his eyes look almost black. His face is sharper, more angled, the stubble on his jaw darker.

He stands out. I think he always will, no matter where he is. He's wearing jeans and a long-sleeved shirt with the sleeves pushed up, exposing his thick forearms. There is writing on his forearms. Big, black letters that blend into the shadows so I cannot read them.

The men who frequent this place do not get tattoos. At least not visible ones. No, these men have polished hands and pressed shirts and impeccable manners.

They don't stand in the doorway, staring.

No, Josh is none of those things. He's not polished and he's not pressed.

Graham slides up beside me and, of course, he has noticed exactly who I'm watching. "Oh, look who's back," Graham murmurs. "Do you have any condoms?"

I lift one brow and try to pretend that I don't actually know who we're talking about. "Are you serious?"

"Don't even try it," Graham says, patting my cheek. "What did you call him the other morning? Mr. Tall, Dark and Depressed?"

"I thought it was Tall, Dark and Psychotic? And didn't we also agreed that he was bad news?"

Graham is a good egg. The kind of guy friend that every girl needs. When Robert the Douche ripped my heart out, it was Graham who sat up with me, throwing darts at a picture of Robert and eating coffee ice cream and making me laugh until my sides hurt.

Until I was no longer sad and hurt.

"You talked about him being bad news. I, however, chatted him up after you left and I think you should spend some more time on the dark side of life. Oh, and Mr. Sexy and Brooding over there looks like he could rock your world in a shake-the-dust-off kind of way."

I roll my eyes at Graham's reference. He's more concerned about my girl parts getting appropriate amounts of attention than I am these days.

Smiling despite myself, I shake my head and walk away. Graham doesn't understand the way I'm wired. He's always been so sure of who he is.

He's never doubted that the people in his life love him for who he is, not despite of it. And that's saying something considering he came out to his evangelical parents when he was sixteen.

Because I cannot stay away, I make my way to where Josh is still cloaked in shadows. "What can I get for you?"

All business. That's the only way through this interaction. I have to keep some distance between us. I've worked too hard to get where I am to risk screwing it up over a guy. Again.

He looks at me silently, letting the quiet wrap around us until I'm sure we're the only two people in the world. Now that I'm closer, his eyes change from dark and hidden in shadows to light, light green. So light they're almost clear. I've never seen a man's eyes change color before. It's fascinating. They stand out even in the dim lighting of the Baywater. And he's got ridiculously dark lashes. He probably doesn't even realize what that does to the ladies.

I take that back. He probably does. Guys like him always end up with girls like Parker throwing themselves at him. They're both lucky enough to have those options. And yeah, I'm a little jealous over the carefree way I imagine him having sex. With Parker.

His penis probably never lacks for company.

I almost smile at the decidedly not business train of thought. But then I realize that he is watching me, silent and unmoving.

"Are you going to speak?" I finally ask. "Or are we going to stare at each other until one of us blinks?"

His lips twitch, and I really don't need to focus on his bottom lip again.

"You never stand at the bar and bullshit with the other waiters. You're always busy." His voice is warm and smooth, not rough and slurring like that night at the bar. Nor is he fierce and solid like he was in class. No, he is something different now.

"Aren't you the observant one?" I brace my hip against the solid wood door. The cut above his eye is almost healed. "No bar fights tonight?"

"Almost." He tips his chin. "Tried getting a drink, but the company at my usual watering hole isn't very appealing this evening."

"Sounds like you were avoiding unpleasant company."

His mouth curves into a smile then and it's kind of overwhelming how it transforms him. The hard edges melt away and his eyes crinkle at the edges.

"Pretty perceptive, aren't you," he says.

I frown but I'm smiling when I shake my head. "It goes with the territory."

He lifts one broad shoulder and I can't help but notice the way his neck moves. I've always been attracted to strong men. Which is part of the problem, because guys who spend too much time in the gym are generally overcompensating for either a underdeveloped sense of self or a small penis. Sometimes both. It's hard to decouple which way the causal arrow goes.

But I should not be letting the butterflies in my stomach entertain ideas about Josh Douglas. He's trouble. He might be dark and compelling and incredibly sexy, but he's trouble nonetheless.

And wow, can I think about something that is not tangentially related to my lack of a sex life? Graham would be so proud.

Josh swallows but says nothing. Again his neck moves, and all my attention zeroes in on the way his skin slides over the muscles.

Down, girl.

He shifts and folds his arms over his chest.

I reach out.

It's a stupid thing. But my curiosity has gotten the best of me. I urge his arm over so I can see the letters those thick black lines form. Both of his forearms are extended now, allowing me to read the stark black letters.

"For I am my brother's keeper," I whisper, reading the words spelled out across the inside of his arms. He shivers beneath my touch. "You didn't strike me as particularly religious."

"I'm not."

"This is a line from the Bible. The book of Genesis, I think."

His eyes have darkened but he hasn't pulled away, leaving his arm resting in my palm.

"The verse references when God asks Cain about his brother Abel." He grinds his teeth, the muscles in his jaw pulsing, his shoulders tense. "I modified it a little bit."

I trace my nail over the word "keeper". "Are you?" I whisper. I am terrified by the powerful want drawing me closer to him.

"Not a very good one." His words are thick and rough. Laced with something I cannot possibly understand.

I swallow because the way he's looking at me…no one has ever looked at me like that before. Like I'm needed. Like I matter. Not what I can do for someone else, but just for me.

It's a stupid craving. A holdover from a time when I was less aware of how the world really works.

There's a flash of disappointment in his eyes. Only a moment and then it's gone but I've been watching people long enough that I notice. What the hell could he be disappointed about?

"Do you get a break?"

"In about a half hour." I glance at my watch. "Are you okay?" I finally ask.

He looks down at my hands, then back up at me. It is strange to be talking to someone and not being mentally undressed. "I don't know."

I think that is the most honest answer anyone has ever given me. And I have no idea what to do with it.

I'm no stranger to really bad shit. It's just that it's usually something I can handle. College drama, mostly, since I've been here. But back home? Before

Dad died and my mom started on the not-so-brief period that we don't talk about? Yeah, sometimes those memories creep in, like they're doing right now.

But Josh is not my nightmare.

At the very least, he deserves a chance to disappoint me all on his own.

I meet his gaze and there is an intensity in his eyes that draws me closer to the flame.

And despite the fear, despite the uncertainty, I am one step closer to the fire.

Chapter Seven

Josh

I don't know why I couldn't find something funny to say. Something to break up the tension and make her laugh. I used to be good at making people laugh. My buddy Mike used to tell me I could make everyone laugh in the middle of a roadside bomb.

I'm fiddling with my phone when Abby steps out of the Baywater. I should have left. Should have gone home and slept everything off. Got up and done it all again tomorrow.

Except that when I'm around her, I feel...alive.

And as she walks toward me, I feel it again. That slow draw back to the light.

I like watching her walk. It's a stupid thing to enjoy, but there is a gentle sway of her hips, a confidence in her steps that is at once feminine and strong. I wonder if she realizes how stunningly beautiful she is. She's not some soft-spoken little mouse, asking for permission to be who she is. There's something about how she walks with her head high, her chin lifted. I love the way the light from the streetlamp bathes her skin in a dusky glow.

I can't explain it but I'm drawn to her. Have been from the moment I saw her.

Maybe it was my time in the Army, but I find a woman with confidence sexy as hell, even when I'm wishing that I was crawling back into a bottle instead of losing the faint buzz I'd managed earlier. All these little girls walking around campus in damn near nothing couldn't hold a candle to Abby with her quick smile and sharp mind.

I wonder what she'd say if I told her that. She'd probably knee me in the balls. And despite them being completely useless, I'm rather partial to them remaining where they are.

She approaches slowly. Almost like she's trying to figure out what she's doing. A tiny silver hoop earring catches the light. I'm not sure why I notice it but I do. It curves around the edge of her earlobe and I'm suddenly tempted to nibble on it.

Yeah, that's called sexual assault, last time I checked. At least it was according to every mandatory sexual assault prevention class I ever attended. There's something wrong with the world when we need a class to teach soldiers how not to rape each other.

And how is that for a buzz killing of a train of thought?

She slows as she approaches. Hesitant now.

"I have to admit, I'm kind of surprised." Her voice is husky and dark. She looks tired and beautiful.

"At what?"

"That you're here."

"I..." I rub the back of my neck. "I can't really think of anything cool or insightful to say that isn't going to make me look like a stalker."

That's mostly true. I don't know why I'm here. Why I'm drawn to her like I am.

I should be honest with her. I should tell her that I'm damaged goods. That I'm unfixable and unfuckable. Maybe I'll see if she wants to cuddle and offer to draw her a puppy or something.

The reality of my world squeezes my throat and makes it difficult to breathe.

"Hey?" There's caution in her voice now. A wariness that I never expected from her. She is too strong, too confident. The hesitation in her voice is at odds with everything I like about her.

I swallow and find my courage. Because I've come all the way here and I'm not going to surrender to the past and slink away like a fucking coward.

"So I just...I guess I just wanted to see if you wanted someone to walk home with you." I didn't plan on asking her that. I didn't actually plan on showing up at all.

But anything is better than letting the walls of my apartment close in on me in the long hours between midnight and dawn.

She tips her head and studies me, her eyes curious. Her lips are soft and curved, and I have a stupid desire to touch her there, to feel if they're as soft as they look. Maybe I'll make easy conversation by asking her what she uses on them. Because I'm trying to get in touch with my inner-metrosexual.

"You came all the way here to ask me if I wanted to walk home with you?"

I lift both eyebrows. That wasn't the response I was looking for, but I suppose it's better than go fuck yourself. "Um, yes?" She's laughing at me. I'm almost certain she's laughing at me. "Why is that so hard to believe?"

"You're a healthy, red blooded American male in an eligible dating market, and instead of being out looking for the future Mrs. Douglas, you're here to see if I want to walk home? Like there's no ulterior motive of trying to get me into bed?"

"Well, stalking is always a course of action for the try-to-get-you-into-bed thing." I honestly can't believe I just said that, but she laughs so maybe it wasn't a disaster. "But it's generally frowned upon, so hopefully I won't have to resort to that."

Her eyes sparkle a little and her lips are quirked at the edges. "That's really not funny."

"Not even a little bit?"

She cocks her head at me, and yes, that's a cautious smile on her full, dark lips. "Have you ever been stalked?"

"Yeah, actually I was once. This girl gave me her number, and like the dumb horny jackass that I was, I called her. Little did I know that she had a history of, ah, being a little clingy."

That's putting it nicely.

"Clingy?"

"I found her in my room, stark naked, one morning after I'd gone for a run. The guys on the hall were less than impressed when she ran down the hallway screaming that she couldn't live without me."

Abby's smiling now, the last trace of uneasiness drifting away. "You're making that up."

"Do I look like I'm making that up?"

"Mighty high opinion of yourself if you expect me to believe you have skinny little white girls throwing their naked bodies at you and you're upset by it," she says dryly.

"What can I say? I'm a great catch."

She shakes her head but she's smiling. "Did you really come here to walk me home?" Her words are quiet, sliding through the darkness to caress my skin with a promise of pleasures that I can no longer feel.

"Maybe I just wanted your number and was too afraid to ask for it outright."

She tips her chin in that way she does. The way that makes me think she sees through all of my bullshit and the lies that I've been hiding behind since I started trying to pretend to be a normal college student.

She surprises me and takes a single step into my space and cups my cheek. Her palm is warm and smooth against my jaw, her fingertips brush against my skin. "You're not like everyone else around here, are you?" she whispers.

"I like to think I blend in."

"You most assuredly do not blend in." Heavy words, laced with potential. I capture her hand beneath mine, holding her there. She's the softest thing I've touched in…I can't remember.

"Is that a good thing or a bad thing?" I can barely breathe.

She's standing a little too close. I want to reach out and pull her against me and feel her softness surround me.

I want.

In a way I haven't wanted in a very long time.

I want the normalcy of this moment, the normalcy of life untouched by war and violence and hate and regrets.

I should let her go. Walk away and pretend that this was a mistake.

But the soft warmth of her skin draws me closer. I'm like a man coming in from the cold, seeing the warmth of a glowing fire.

A better man would walk away.

But I am not a better man.

Abby

My heart is pounding. I don't know how to do this. Things like this don't come easy to me. With Robert, everything was pretty rational. I remember being so glad I wasn't alone. That someone found me desirable.

It was a nice fantasy while it lasted.

"I think it's a good thing," I whisper. I can't say

what made me touch him. What made me reach across that space and press my palm to his cheek.

But with Josh, nothing makes sense. He captures my hand and there is no pulling away.

There is a hesitation between us. Something tangible and real that keeps me from closing the gap.

And then he moves. The barest hint of movement. His lips brush against mine. His breath is warm on my skin, luring me closer to everything that is Josh.

I want in a way I've never wanted before. My heart pounds in my ears and everything I am is focused on Josh. The feel of his hand on mine. His scent is a mixture of spice and leather. It draws me closer, wrapping around me like a warm summer day.

This. This is what it must feel like to be wanted. To feel like you are the center of someone's entire universe.

His lips are softer than I expected. A gentle, hesitant trust in that tentative gesture. He is warm and smooth and strong. Questioning.

I shift, wanting to open, wanting to deepen the kiss. Wanting more of the delicious sensation purring over my skin and through my veins. Wanting to push aside the doubt and the terrible memories that push me away from anything good in my life.

His other hand comes up and cups my cheek. Here, he is as rough and rugged as I expected. His hands are not manicured and covered in lotion. They are strong and calloused and completely at odds with everything I am.

I want more. I want very much to go into the darkness with this man and let the world fall away.

A small noise escapes me. Maybe it's desire. Maybe it's want or need in that tiny sound.

I don't expect him to notice. Most guys are pretty tone deaf to that kind of stuff.

But he does. His fingers tense against my skin, a reflexive touch that tells me more about the strength of his own reaction than any words could have.

In an instant, he shifts back, creating space between us. "Sorry," he mumbles.

I want to tell him no, it's okay and please touch me again.

But I can't find the words. They're too heavy, too filled with my own inadequacy and shame for not being strong enough to take what he's offering.

"Don't apologize," I whisper. It is as close to reassuring as I can manage. I'm not sure I could say anything more even if I wanted to.

He swallows and lowers his hand. "I, ah, the offer to walk you home still stands. You know, if you'd like some company."

There is such a sharp sense of loss beating in time with my heart now that I have to get away. I can't do this, no matter how much I might want to. Josh is one of the good ones. Which means I am guaranteed to screw it up somehow.

"Thank you," I whisper. I reach up and cup his cheek. "It's sweet of you to offer." I hesitate. "But I'm meeting friends after work tonight."

I wish it were a lie. I wish I could meet him later and explore the paths and hidden potential in that kiss. But I don't abandon my friends for the first hint of my blood running hot for a guy. "I've got to get back to work." Regret, honest and simple, in that simple sentence.

"Abby?" His voice is a quiet whisper in the darkness.

I turn back, looking over my shoulder at the man cast in shadows and light. "Yeah?"

"Thank you."

"For what?"

He hesitates. "For everything."

And he is gone, leaving me standing there wondering at the complex mystery that is Josh Douglas.

Chapter Eight

Josh

I don't actually sleep. It doesn't count as sleep if you lie awake in the dark with the room spinning slowly.

I haven't slept well since the war. But I can't tell anyone that. It's not like I'm ashamed of it or anything. It's...If it wasn't for Eli and the guys, I'd probably be a hell of a lot worse off than I am.

My attempt to distract myself away from the burning memories tonight fell flat when Abby begged off a walk home.

It's not her fault. Who just shows up at someone's work and says Me Man, You Woman. Me walk you home. And expect everything to go swimmingly.

But the lack of a distraction means I've got to figure some shit out or the rest of the night is going to get real froggy real quick. So instead of heading home, I head to the campus fitness center.

I strip and change into my gym clothes, which I keep in a locker I rent for six dollars a month. It's easier than carrying that stuff around with me every time I come on campus, and luckily, tuition comes with a fee for the fitness center that us non-athletes get to use when the Division One teams aren't using them.

I hit the treadmill and take off at a slow jog. I no longer have to keep up with my division commander, who liked to run marathons for funsies. I thought he was going to kill me on multiple occasions. It was strange how he kept me around. I was his driver. I should have been out running around with the other drivers, but instead, he had me shadowing his aide de camp and keeping him in line.

Damn it. I'm running to avoid the memories or at least run them into exhaustion and instead I crash right into them.

I crank up the speed on the treadmill.

But still. All I can see are Mike's boots. He'd been standing in them a few minutes before. The tan leather is stained with blood.

We used to joke about what we'd do when we made it home from war. I remember just wanting to get laid.

Mike had just wanted to see his dog. She was some kind of giant Labrador or something.

I wonder if his mom still has her. Or if the dog even knows Mike is never coming home.

Christ, but I don't want to think about Mike. I don't want to think about the goddamned war and the anger and the rage and how fucking good it felt to unleash hell that day.

Or the shame that washes over me every single time I think about that godawful day.

I crank the treadmill up again. Trying to find my rhythm. Trying to find a way to outrun the blood and memories and crash into a fatigue that will force me to sleep. The pounding of my feet on the tread, my heart in my ears.

It's easy enough to pretend I'm back at Hood, my last duty station, running down Battalion Avenue, a hundred of us in step and in sync. There's nothing in the world better than falling into the formation and feeling like you've stepped into something else entirely.

God but I miss those days. Hard. I didn't think I would. I thought I'd be glad not to get up and head out the door to PT at the ass crack of dawn anymore.

Never thought I'd miss it.

Not after everything.

Except that now, I'd give anything if she'd take me back. I'd even bear the shame of everything if only I could spend one more day in the shit and the sand and the dirt. Laughing with Mike. Bitching about the heat.

I'd do anything.

But I can't go back. I can't give in to the darkness and the temptation the Army offers. And there's not a damn thing I can do about it.

And so I run. I fall into the memories of running in formation and pretend that I still belong somewhere out there in the world. That there is a place for me where I fit.

Because right now, I'm not sure that such a place exists. And I am terrified of the fact that I am completely and utterly alone.

I run until sweat pours down my spine and soaks my clothing. I run until my legs burn and I'm just this side of throwing up.

I run until I no longer see Mike's boots or the blood on my hands or the twisted joy I felt every time I pulled the trigger that day.

I run until it dawns on me that I can't keep running.

It is a long moment before I step into the shower. I let the steam blast my body, hands braced against the wall, and I make a decision.

I want. I want to belong. I want to do my job again. I want to make a difference. I want to believe that what I'm doing matters.

I want to stop fucking feeling like this. Like I'm buried, moving through life in muted slow motion.

I close my eyes and double over.

I want the fucking war to let me go.

Abby

I've got thirty minutes to get my assignment done for Quinn's class on violence. I should have done it during break last night but I didn't. I can't afford to let my grades slide. It puts my financial aid at risk.

Given that I want to work with at-risk women, my advisor recommended I take Quinn's class to better understand what happens to people in violent situations.

I don't want to tell her that I know all too well what happens in these situations. But if I mention it, then I risk chipping away at the got-it-together façade that I've worked so hard to maintain.

It's a mask that's slipped recently.

Okay, it didn't slip. It was pried away with the carefully placed knife Robert the Douche slipped beneath the defenses that I'd built up so carefully since I'd started school.

I give myself a quick shake and push that memory out of my mind. It's too easy to blame Robert for the unraveling, but it's not all Robert's fault.

He's a symptom, not the disease. My fingers start flying on my keyboard, my response flowing as though it happened to someone else.

Interpersonal violence is a difficult situation to understand. Part of this comes from misunderstanding the nature of the problem. If being involved in a violent relationship was the result of rational decision making, no one would ever be involved in violence; either as victim or as perpetrator.

"You look deep in thought."

Josh's voice slides out of the silence of the library and wraps around me. I look up from my assignment. He is standing there in the bright overhead lights, looking just as out of place here as he does in the Baywater.

The responsible part of me should be annoyed because now I have to be sociable when I have to get my assignment done.

But another part of me is doing a happy dance in my panties.

Down, girl.

"How's the eye?" The shiner is faded now, an ugly yellow and green, the scab mostly gone at this point. On campus, it's rare to see someone who's not an athlete walking around with a bruised face. But beyond that, this one distracts me because it pulls my attention straight to Josh and only Josh.

And that's dangerous for me.

I don't want to feel anything for him. For anyone. Maybe someday. But not today.

"Better. Not sore anymore." I like the way he looks at me. Like he can see me. Not the stereotype everyone else seems to see.

Me.

"What?"

"Sorry," I mumble. Damn it, he caught me staring. "I was distracted."

I'm trying not to notice. Not his shoulders or the hard, clean lines of his collarbones and the little indent at the base of his throat. And the solid line of muscle that is his chest that makes me really want to get a little bit naked.

"By what?"

Shit. I need something witty and smart. Except that I'm not witty and smart. At least, not under pressure.

"Your ass."

Which I suppose is close enough to the truth to

make him doubt that it is actually the truth. Did I mention I was terrible at reverse psychology, too?

A tiny crease forms at the edge of his mouth. I look away from the distinctly not-academic turn of my thoughts and the dangerous glint in Josh's eye. Suddenly, I very much think he is not doubting the truth of my response. How's that for a plan backfiring?

He makes a noise in his throat, and I very much remember the feel of his lips against mine.

"Careful. I might think you're flirting with me." I love the sound of his voice.

I want to feel him again. His taste, the softness of his mouth on mine. The rough scrape of his stubble against my skin.

"I have an assignment due."

I look away. This isn't going very smoothly at all. I can't do this again. Not right now. And no, the parts of my anatomy that are currently standing up at attention at his proximity do not get a vote.

For a big man covered in tattoos, he surprises me with the vulnerability I see looking back at me, hidden behind a teasing smile.

"So what you're saying is that I might have a better shot next week? Or after your assignment is done?"

I smile despite myself. Clearly, reason is not going to work with him. Or my own damn hormones. Traitorous bastards. "You're not listening."

"No, I am. In fact, I'll show you exactly how good I can listen." He snaps his fingers. "I'll be back in a few minutes."

"Why a few minutes?"

"Because judging by how fast you were typing a minute ago, the faster you get your assignment done, the faster I get to have you checking out my sweet ass."

And damn it, I laugh as he up and walks away toward the coffee shop in the library.

Because sure enough, he looks over his shoulder.

Just in time to see me checking out his ass.

I am so screwed.

Chapter Nine

Josh

I didn't actually have a plan when I walked up to Abby. I just saw her sitting there and was hit with a sense of longing, a sense of being found that was so strong, so compelling, there was little I could have done to ignore it.

I can't stop thinking about the way she felt beneath my lips. The way she yielded beneath my touch as I kissed her. And when she'd opened, just a little, the want inside me damn near dropped me to my knees. She made me miss things I'd given up on. Things I thought I'd made peace with, the way my life had turned out.

I was wrong.

I hadn't meant to kiss her. To think about her. To start looking for her in a crowd. It had just kind of happened. Kind of like how I'd ended up at the Baywater to begin with.

My small obsession isn't going anywhere any time soon. But given that she just told me she was checking out my sweet ass, and then I caught her doing exactly that, my day was looking up.

It felt good to tease her. Like I was stepping into the sunshine after a long grey period. It had been so long since I'd been around a female who I was genuinely attracted to. I don't count the bullshit hookups back at Hood. Or my stalker.

I order coffee, and because I have no idea what she might actually want, I stuff a bunch of cream and sugar in my pocket. I count to one hundred before I go back to where she's sitting.

"I managed to stay away for five minutes." I set the coffee down next to her computer. "Was it long enough?"

She looks away from her computer at me. Her eyes are liquid gold in the light, lined with a darker sable ring. And yeah, I've got it fucking bad if I'm noticing her irises.

If I close my eyes, I can see her standing next to me at the bar, her eyes dark and concerned. As though I mattered.

Like she really saw me and not the pretense I've been showing the world since I got back from the war.

She glances at the coffee cup in my hand. "What if I don't drink coffee?"

"Well, ah...I hope you'll be polite and drink it anyway because, otherwise, my notoriously fragile male ego might shatter into a thousand pieces. I might never recover from the rejection." I dump the cream and sugar packets on the table then look up at her, suddenly deeply unsure that I might have offended her. "Do you drink coffee?"

She laughs, and it's a full laugh, not some insipid giggle.

"Yeah, Josh, I drink coffee." She opens a creamer. "Thank you for this."

"Well, if your night was anything like mine, you're going to have a hell of a time staying awake in Quinn's class today." I watch her dump all the cream and half the sugar into her coffee. "Want a little coffee with your cream?"

"You are not allowed to judge my caffeine preferences." She points that little stir stick in my face.

"You could never be in the Army," I say. "We can't run without caffeine, but half the time all we have is that instant coffee creamer."

She looks down at her coffee, her expression darkening just a little.

It takes me a second to realize what I've said.

Fuck. I clear my throat. "You don't have a moral objection to soldiers or anything, do you?"

I don't advertise that I'm a soldier. I don't hide it, either, but some supposedly educated people have strong moral objections to the Army. Oh, everyone will smile and say "thank you for your service" and all the while be thinking we're just poor dumb bastards who should have gone to college in the first place.

Please don't be one of them.

"No," she says quietly. "My dad used to drink his coffee black or with some of that fake creamer. It was so gross."

I hesitate, unsure how we went from coffee to her

father but I'm sure there's a connection. "Used to?"

She pauses where she's stirring her drink. "He died in the war."

I'm not sure what shocks me more: the fact that Abby has a connection to the Army I've been running away from and back to at the same time, or the news that her dad died in the war.

"I'm sorry," I whisper. Because there is nothing appropriate to say. Nothing that will make it okay or ease the pain.

And the pain never goes away. Ever.

Her throat moves and she intently finishes stirring her coffee. "I was little. It's funny. I can remember the sound of his laugh. And I remember the coffee. But I have a hard time remembering what he looks like if I don't have a picture of him."

"Do you have one?" I'm suddenly insanely curious about her parents.

She turns her computer toward me. A pretty young white woman who looks exactly like Abby stands looking up at a powerful-looking black man in a uniform similar to Army uniforms but definitely not Army. Between them is a beautiful little girl with shiny bronze skin and a brilliant smile and curly brown hair in two poofs on the top of her head: Abby. "He was a Marine." Not Army like I'd assumed.

"A sergeant major?"

She smiles. "He was."

"How old were you in that picture?"

"Seven."

"Shit, Abby."

"Like I said, I don't remember much about him."

She's being way too nonchalant about this but I can't push her right then without being an asshole. "You look like you were happy."

"We were." She pauses. "You're not going to comment on my parents?"

"What's to comment on?"

She lifts an eyebrow. "Really?"

"It's not 1968 anymore."

"You're not going to give me any of that 'I don't see color' bullshit, are you?" She's trying to make light of it but I can feel the tension radiating off her now. The teasing mood from earlier is gone, and I did that by asking stupid questions.

I do the only thing I can think of. I cup her cheek gently, sliding my thumb over her beautiful dark skin. "I see you, Abby. I see everything about you."

Her lips part. A quiet gasp. I've never been very good with words but at that moment, I feel like I hit a home fucking run. I can feel the shift in her. The strange transfer of energy from one tension to another.

One that draws me closer to her until her mouth is a breath from mine. I want so badly to brush my lips against hers. To taste her and see if she'll lean a little bit closer.

I hesitate because, with Abby, I feel like I'm always one step away from fucking up royally. I lean in, slowly, so slowly, never breaking my gaze away from hers. Her pulse scatters beneath my fingertips.

I brush my lips against hers. Give her time to pull away. Time to react if this is not something she wants.

She's fully in charge here. Fully able to rip my heart out of my chest and grind it into the ground.

But she doesn't. For a moment, only a moment, she leans into me. Her lips brush against mine, a ghost of a sensation, the barest caress. Her breath is warm on my mouth. I want to breathe her in. Taste her.

Take her somewhere where it's just her and just me, and I can spend all afternoon just kissing her.

Her touch is the faintest glimpse of heaven after a lifetime in hell.

Abby

I lean into him. It is all at once the stupidest thing I've done in a long time and the most compelling. I cannot move away. I'm not sure I want to. His hand is rough against my skin. Rough but infinitely gentle. And before I can think about what I'm doing, I open beneath his mouth and close that final distance between us.

His lips are full and smooth. I can almost feel him exhale. It's a physical change in him, where he relaxes into me. I can't say how I know it, but I feel it in everything that I am. I brace one hand on his thigh to keep from crashing into him and open a little more, inviting his touch, his taste.

Inviting disaster because that's what this is.

But he's far too tempting to walk away from. My tongue slides against his, and a tremble runs through him and into me. My breath hitches as he deepens the kiss, and I open until he is surrounding me, consuming me, and all I want to do is crawl into his lap and let the world stop around us.

He makes a warm noise in his throat, and his hand slides over my cheek and down my throat to cradle my neck. I feel cherished and such a keening sense of want that it physically burns inside me, reminding me of things I can't have.

I gently, so gently, ease back.

"Well," I say. "That was certainly unexpected."

He lowers his forehead to mine and laughs.

"Jesus, you're hell on the ego," he whispers against my mouth. I hear an echo of something harsh and cruel that Robert said to me once, but I don't stiffen. I refuse to let Robert into my head to ruin this.

I cup his cheek gently. "Unexpected in a good way."

"What about in a 'I'd like to do that again sometime' way?" His voice is low and heavy. I can imagine him in bed, his long body pressed against mine, his words as much of a caress as his fingers or his tongue.

I close my eyes. I have a thousand reasons to hesitate. Even more to run in the opposite direction.

There are no happily ever afters for girls like me.

Girls who can't keep their mouths shut and go along with society's expectations of what a good girl is. And it hurts, it physically hurts, to think of how this ends.

Because it will end. It always does.

"Hey?"

I open my eyes, not realizing that I hadn't responded. "I've probably done irreparable damage to your ego at this point, haven't I?"

He smiles. "I'm a little bit tougher than that. Not much, though." He brushes his thumb over my bottom lip. "You don't have to answer."

I narrow my eyes then. "You're quite the mystery, aren't you?"

"I suppose?"

Because I can't help it, I lean in, brushing my lips across his. "You're like a good dream. And I don't want to wake up."

He grins but there is a shadow in his eyes. "There's something to be said for good dreams."

"That's an odd thing to say," I whisper against his mouth.

Josh Douglas is a craving. A want.

And he's turning into an unhealthy distraction from my purpose here at school. Oh, I want to do this. Him. I really do. Josh has a whole lot of good going for him. And that's before I mentally strip that shirt from his body and explore those glorious shoulders with my fingers.

He shrugs and shifts so that he's resting his elbows on his knees. The tattoos on his forearms are more than shadows now. I am drawn to the stark lines on his skin. "Why these words?"

I swallow and physically move closer. Apparently, I'm about as subtle as an elephant in the room because he notices my eyes drop to his arms.

"You have a thing for tattoos?" he asks.

I don't want to answer. I don't want to resurrect anything about those memories that are circling dangerously, waiting for the right moment to strike.

"Not really." The truth, from a certain point of view. From another point of view, though, it's terrifyingly simple. And it's a simplicity that I'm not ready to talk to him—or anyone—about. "I'm curious, that's all."

It doesn't matter anymore. It does not get a vote on who I am anymore.

"I got them before my last deployment," he says after a moment.

I blink rapidly, the lines on his arms blurring as a memory hits me hard. "So are you?" I look up at him. "Your brother's keeper?"

"I was." He swallows hard and looks away. "I'm not anymore." He looks back at me.

"Who are you?"

He says nothing. People say you can't change what you come from. They might be right but that doesn't mean you have to let it define you. You don't have to keep going back home again and taking shit from people about how much better you think you are than they are now that you've got an education.

And holy shit I am not doing this. I can't wait for

his response. I can't let myself be drawn toward the darkness.

I have to focus. I have to keep moving forward before the past catches up to me and drags me back where I come from. To a place where tattoos are drunkenly etched into hard, damaged skin. Where life is nasty, brutish, and short.

I lift my laptop to my knees. "I really need to finish my assignment." The truth, cloaked in regret. "I'm on scholarship. I have to keep my grades up."

I don't miss the flicker of disappointment a moment before he smiles.

It doesn't reach his eyes.

I lick my lips, wishing I couldn't taste him on me. I can smell him on my skin from that brief contact. And I want more, so much more.

But Robert destroyed a lot in those few months. He destroyed the façade that I'd built out of the wreckage of an out-of-place kid from southern Georgia who didn't belong at a wealthy college. He reminded me that this is not my world and that no matter how hard I try, I will never truly fit here.

I can feel my past pulling at me, trying to drag me back down to what I was. Angry. Withdrawn. Hating the world.

I will not be that person again.

When Josh gets up to leave, I don't stop him.

Proving that the insecure person I was is very much a part of who I am.

Chapter Ten

Josh

I can't go to class. I feel sick to my stomach. It's twisting and knotted and wrenching.

I'd been there. For a moment, I'd been in that space where I could flirt with a beautiful woman and pretend that there was nothing more to me than a few tattoos and a tendency toward moodiness.

And then it ended. Just like that, it was over and I couldn't find my way back to the space we'd been in where we'd just been two normal people.

I'm at The Pint. I'm arguably trying to think about my homework, but the idea of trying to dissect the violence from a surgical distance—makes me physically ill.

"You look like hell."

Eli drops a stack of papers on the bar. "Pot meet kettle."

If I look like I had one too many last night—which I did—Eli looks like he hasn't slept in a week. Which he might not have.

"It's been a rough week." The weight of those words hits me hard.

"What's wrong?"

I pick the easiest problem. One that a bartender is probably used to hearing from fellow vets. "I can't sleep."

It sounds like such a simple thing. Such an elegant, simple thing, but sleep is the most important thing. More important than love. More important than sex.

He leans on the bar. "When did you sleep last?"

"About three hours last night. A couple the night before."

"Have you talked to your doc?"

I make a rude noise. "I'm over my allocation of visits, according to the VA."

"No sleep meds?"

I shrug and lean back. "They don't work anymore. One of the guys at the VA told me when they stop working, you're all kinds of fucked up." I look down at my phone. The screen is black and silent. "I had a sergeant major once who ate Ambien like Tic Tacs."

"Has anything worked since you came home?"

Shame flashes over my skin. He's been there for a lot of it. But he'd never guess why I really fought. I could tell him. Let the words slip.

Instead, I back away. Finding the safest answer. "I guess I'm used to getting a couple of hours of sleep now." There is resignation in the pit of my belly, coupled with relief. Maybe I've been hiding things too long. Maybe…

I shake my head, unwilling to resurrect the secrets I've been trying to ignore since I came home. And I'm trying, really fucking trying, to avoid the seductive lure of the bottle.

It's hard not being a neurotic train wreck these days. I mean, it's not like I've got a hell of a lot of reassurances that I'm able to walk in this world and pretend I'm a normal fucking human being.

What can I tell him about Abby? How do I admit that I've found a girl I'm over the fucking moon about, but can't do anything about it?

"I met a girl."

"And this is complicated because…?"

"It's complicated."

Eli lifts one brow and folds his arms over his chest. I swear to God, I can't see him as an officer. Maybe a first sergeant. But not as my commander. "It's not complicated. Boy meets girl. Boy fucks girl. If boy is good in the sack, girl decides she wants to see boy again. If not, she doesn't call. It's really as simple as that."

Heat crawls up my neck at his words.

Eli frowns. "You're not a virgin, are you? Is that what the problem is? You don't know how to use your dick?"

"That's not exactly what the problem is."

He leans back against the bar. "Now I'm confused."

I can't say it. I trust him—it's not that I worry he'll tell that dickbag Caleb or anyone else for that matter.

It's that the words are stuck in my throat. That

they represent a truth about my life that I'm in denial about. "I can't, ah…" I can't say it.

His mouth falls open after a moment. "Holy shit, you can't…you haven't…" He hesitates. "How long?"

"More than a year."

"You try Viagra or anything like it?"

"No, I've been suffering in silence when a little blue pill will fix everything. Of course I fucking tried it." I need a goddamned drink.

"Docs?"

"Have no explanation for it other than it's anxiety."

"Then maybe you need to relax a little bit."

I press my lips together. This conversation isn't really going how I planned it. Not that I planned it. How the hell did my psychoses end up as the topic of conversation?

"You tell her?"

"Yeah, sure. Hi, my name is Josh and I think you're really fucking hot, but hey, my dick doesn't work so you know, we can maybe cuddle and I'll draw you a picture of a kitten or something." I narrow my eyes when he laughs. "It's not fucking funny."

"It is when you put it that way."

"Thanks."

He slides a beer across the bar. At least he's a fucking mind reader. "You like this girl. Just be honest with her."

"It's not that simple."

"Yeah, actually it is. Ninety-nine percent of all

relationship problems are caused by lack of communication." He pauses, his expression sobering. "Look, I know I'm jerking your chain. But maybe figuring out how to talk to this chick about this might not be a bad idea. Take some of the performance anxiety out of the equation." He drags one hand over his head. "I'm assuming this hasn't been brought up, either? With docs? About the war or anything?"

"Nah. I gave up after the first time when they gave me the Viagra. Just you guys here. That's all I need." I look away from my phone, toward the door of the bar, hoping that Abby would by some miracle walk through the door and chase away the uncertainty that's making me crazy. "Why did you start this place up here? I mean, it's a college town. There aren't that many of us around here."

He dumps ice into an orange glass pitcher. Because plastic wouldn't be eclectic enough. Not for this town. "That's exactly why. There are plenty of places for guys like us to hang our hats down at Bragg or back at Hood. But here? There are more of us here than people realize. And we need each other. We always will." He looks toward the door. "No one else gets it when you talk about not being able to feel close to the person you love. Or why your temper just snaps for no fucking reason." He hesitates. "Or understands when your dick doesn't work, that it's not actually as simple as a little Viagra mixed with porn to fix what ails you." He looks back at me. "And I didn't want to be around all the shitbag wannabes running their mouths down at Bragg about what they did. I wanted to be somewhere where what I did matters."

He sounds like my old platoon sergeant. "Man, you sure you weren't an NCO in another life?"

Eli shakes his head. "Nah. That was my dad." He places two shot glasses on the counter. "Why are you all freaked out about this girl?"

Pale golden liquid splashes on the bar as he fills the glasses.

"She's…special."

"Clearly. Otherwise you wouldn't be sitting here moping because you can't get it up and you're letting it ruin your relationship before it even gets started." He pours a shot for both of us. At this rate, I'll be asleep in an hour. Which is good. Because when I pass out, I don't have any dreams that twist into nightmares.

You don't really appreciate sleep until you don't have a choice to have it on a regular basis.

"I'm a little bit fucked up," I admit after I choke down the second shot.

"Aren't we all?"

I shake my head. "Not like that." I can't say the words. I can't put the psychological bullshit into words.

The docs said it was temporary. That it wouldn't last.

But it's been a year.

A fucking year since I felt anything but a shadow of my former self.

I hold out the shot glass and Eli refills it. Because that's the kind of friend Eli has become. It's a slow burn this time, sliding through my veins with liquid heat.

"I'm not going to judge. We all have to confront our shit when we're ready," he says.

I look up at him again. "What if we're never ready?"

"Then do what you can. And hope that you can lighten the load enough that the stuff you can't offload doesn't get too heavy."

"Have you?"

"Have I what?" he asks, pouring a fourth shot for each of us. Man but he can fucking drink. I'm going to start slurring soon.

"Unpacked everything."

He shakes his head slowly. "Not even close."

I look down into the empty shot glass. There's a tiny amount of liquid gold at the bottom and it makes me think of Abby's dark golden eyes.

I wish she was here. Close enough to feel her heart beating beneath my palm, her hair soft against my cheek. I want to wake up with her in my arms and hold her as I fall asleep.

And I can't. I'll never be able to love her right.

And she deserves better than that.

Abby

Class has been cancelled for the last two days—oddly enough, due to unknown reasons. The running theory is that Quinn ate some bad cilantro at one of the local chain restaurants. Cue smugness that he should have been eating locally, from several of my classmates.

Either way, it bought me time to figure out what to do with the twisted mess inside me where Josh is concerned.

Because make no mistake—there is a mess.

I close my eyes, regret bolting through me that I ran him off.

"You look like hell."

I open my eyes to see Graham standing in the doorway of the break room. He's normally perky and upbeat on the worst of days but right now, he's got a look around him that I've come to know all too well. "And you look like you just hooked up."

He grins wickedly. "Maybe I've met a vegan body builder."

"And Mr. Wonderful rocked your world?"

"Very much so." And Graham does something a little unexpected. He blushes—and Graham is about the most confident, non-blushing person I know.

"Oh, this is getting a little serious, isn't it?" I ask. It's easy to be happy for Graham. He's got more reasons than most to be jaded and cynical, but he's not. And I think that's one of the things I love about him.

He helps me feel like I belong here and has from the very start, when I was ashamed to have to be working my way through this university, where the poor kids drive Mercedes and the really rich ones have drivers.

I pull myself back from my mental meanderings to find him watching me. "There's something you're not telling me," he says. "Does it involve Mr. Tall, Dark and Psychotic?"

I duck my head, not sure how to answer. "In a roundabout way, yeah."

He moves across the room like a ghost and is suddenly sitting across from me. "Do tell."

"He's just... There's something about him." I twist my hair absently, redoing a few curls that have gotten away from me lately. "The other night when he was at the Baywater? He wanted to walk me home."

"And you said no, didn't you?"

"Yeah, guy totally shows up at work out of the blue and asks to walk me home and I'm going to jump all over it. That's how horror movies start."

"That's also how pornos start," he says. "And lord knows this dry spell of yours has gone on long enough."

"I've seen that movie," I say quietly.

"Not the one with this guy as the star." He slides into the chair next to me. "Look, I don't get the creepy stalker vibe from him. You should give it a shot. Even if it's just for coffee."

"Is coffee a euphemism for sex?"

"Well, you know, oral is known as flicking the bean."

I laugh because I can't help myself. "Really? How do you know these things?"

"I used to steal my mom's Playgirl magazines."

"I really didn't need that visual."

"You're welcome." He drums his fingers on the table in front of him.

I hesitate for a moment, not wanting to risk asking Graham a question I may not really want to know the answer to. "You know he used to be a soldier, right?"

"Yeah. He told me that day at the bar. I guess that explains why he reminds me of Noah," Graham says softly. Noah is a former soldier and is seriously involved with our friend Beth. And he's got a metric ton of issues from the war.

And just like that, I am no longer confident about what I have considered getting myself into with Josh. "I know."

Graham reaches for my hand and squeezes it. "That means that whatever issues he's got, underneath it all, he's a good guy."

I press my lips together. I don't want to be there to pick up the pieces. I've done that before, and it sucks because even when the person you love is standing there, cut and bleeding, a part of you hates them for putting themselves in that situation to begin with.

I know what I've felt every single time I am around Josh. I know how I felt when his mouth touched mine.

I know what I'd be giving up if I walk away from this thing that's starting between me and Josh. It's something I've wanted my entire life.

But the part of me that whispers to run…I can't. I have to stop letting that part of me rule my life. I won't live afraid.

Not even now, when I'm pretty well convinced that I am going to end up just like my mother—hurt and broken and lying on the bedroom floor, crying her eyes out, then crawling back to the bastard that ripped her soul out.

I suddenly do not want to be alone. I very much want to take a chance with Josh.

I want to lay my head on Josh's shoulder. Feel his strong body curled around mine. And I'm afraid of how strongly I feel the pull toward him. Despite the mystery. Despite the darkness. That maybe, just maybe, hope would be enough to pull him through whatever it is that he's facing.

And that maybe, he wants someone to face it with him.

I'm tired of being alone. After Robert, after my dad. After my mom's boyfriend made it all too clear that I was the reason their relationship went to hell.

Too many things are circling in my mind today as I finish my shift at work and head home.

Too many resurrected specters from my past destroying my present.

I have a choice.

I can be safe.

Or I can choose to fall.

Chapter Eleven

Josh

Finally admitting the problem to Eli hasn't solved anything. I should be able to identify the feeling twisting in my guts at this point. I've had lots of time snuggling up with anxiety and its fun cousins panic attack and nausea.

But I can't sit around and mope about it either. Nothing has changed. Which means I need to drag my happy ass to campus and pretend to be normal for another day.

I arrive at class early and disappointment is a tangible thing in my gut when I see that she's not there yet. I take a seat at the back of the small raised rows. I tap my pen on my thigh. Sitting still has never been one of my strong points. It's good for my blood pressure.

I'm watching the door, waiting. Just waiting.

I have no right to feel this...this anticipation. She's not mine. She can't be.

But I can't forget how it felt to kiss her. A momentary breakthrough in my neuroses where for a brief moment, I found the right thing to say, the right thing to do.

I lick my bottom lip, remembering the feel of her mouth beneath mine. That kiss was as close to paradise as I've felt since I came home from the war.

And I want to taste her again.

She is perfection in so many ways. Soft, lush. Warm.

I didn't want to stop. I wanted to keep going, to see if my body could be dragged kicking and screaming back into life. But the kiss hadn't lasted long enough to tease out any stirrings of real desire.

It's been so fucking long since I've felt anything other than a need to do violence. So long since someone did something as simple as touch me.

I am hollow. Violence has been the only thing that makes me feel. But after I kissed Abby? That kiss changed everything and nothing all at once.

Not everything, of course. But I've tasted a promise of something different from the life I've lived.

I'm learning, right? That's what I'm doing here at school. Learning how to do the adult, civilized thing.

To try and find the thing that I'll become without the Army.

So far, college isn't helping with that plan, but hell, I'm only on my second semester here.

My confidence has been shot all to hell since I came home. I know it's something I should go to the doc for. But honestly, I just can't summon the courage or resilience or whatever to put the problem into words again. Because words would make it real.

There's nothing worse than having to explain to

the nurse on the phone that you need an appointment for your dick not working. It's something they expect out of fifty-year-old cardiac arrest patients, not twenty-five-year-old college students.

And talking about it means I risk opening up the box of terrible memories that haunt me in my sleep. I can't do that.

Admitting it would be admitting that the war broke me. That it damaged me in ways I'm not ready to confront.

I need to figure out who I am first.

After that, maybe I can figure out what's wrong with my cock.

My heart slams against my ribs the moment Abby pauses in the doorway of the classroom. Her eyes lock on me. I want to look away. To pretend that she's not the only thing I can see.

But I don't.

I meet her gaze. And answer the questions there with more of my own.

Why did she pull away? What—or rather who—hurt her so badly that she questions her own instincts? Because she'd kissed me. I'd felt her response down to my soul. And then just like that, she was gone. One minute, she's laughing and teasing; the next, she's cool, shutting down.

There has to be more to the story. Because Abby doesn't strike me as the type to play games.

She doesn't look away. Instead, there is a tiny, apologetic smile at the edge of her full, dusky lips. I swallow and do nothing. The ball is in her court, and at this moment, I am powerless to react as she starts climbing the steps to where I'm sitting. Powerless to shut down the flare of hope that rises inside me with every step she takes.

"Can I join you?" Her voice is low and smooth and throaty. Hesitant. As though she expects me to tell her to pound sand.

I lift one eyebrow. I can do this. I can smile and flirt with the pretty girl like a normal guy. "You're not worried about me getting too wound up with the discussion?"

Her lips quirk a little more, and I am aching to touch her. To slide my finger over her bottom lip and feel her breath brush against my fingertip.

"I'll take my chances."

"You like to live dangerously?"

"Sitting with you is not dangerous."

I look at her then, surprised by the naivety in her simple statement. Or maybe it's the sheer simplicity of the faith in those words.

They cut me. Deeply.

Because she has no idea who I am or what I've done. I swallow and force those thoughts away. I will not let the war ruin everything. I have to fight back.

"You don't know me well enough to make that statement." My words are thick. Heavy. Laced with powerful memories that could tear me apart piece by piece if I let them.

This isn't the way to flirt. Damn it.

"I'd like to," she whispers.

I am frozen to the spot. My mouth moves but no

sound comes out. I am paralyzed in the grip of sudden uncertainty.

I want this. I want to cross the space between us and take a chance that I can come back from the fucked up place that I've been since I came home. That I can be normal again. That I can kiss a fucking hot girl and maybe, just maybe, get turned on by something other than violence.

And I am suddenly terrified of falling.

Chapter Twelve

Josh

Professor Quinn surveys the classroom, his expression blank even as his gaze lands on us, then he moves to his podium and opens a well-oiled leather folio. The kind of folio that looks like old money without even trying. "Your assigned readings from this lesson argued that violence was declining around the world. Despite war in the Middle East, various conflicts in Africa, the rise of gang violence in Mexico, just to name a few, the author argued that violence is indeed declining. Do you buy his argument?"

I sit there, studying my pen and the blank sheet of notebook paper in front of me. Half the class has their laptops open to a game or to the latest social media site. I'm a little old-fashioned, I guess.

"Mr. Douglas, what do you think?"

I buy myself a moment by breathing deeply, holding it until my lungs burn, and releasing it. "I don't buy it. His argument doesn't hold up to even the lightest inspection."

Quinn motions toward me with his open palm,

his thumb cradling the presentation remote. "And why don't you buy it? We haven't had a major world conflict since the end of World War II."

I flick the end of my pen off and back on again but Abby interrupts. "True, sir, but he's arguing that violence across the board has decreased. Pointing to the lack of a major global conflict suggests that the level of state-sponsored violence may have declined, but it does not suggest that violence overall has decreased."

I can feel everyone's eyes on us as Quinn digests her answer. Then he nods once. "Very good, Ms. Hilliard. Does anyone want to argue against this?"

Of course, Parker's hand goes up. "Sir, I don't think you can argue that violence isn't declining. We see an overall decline in violent arrests in the United States. The countries of the old Western Europe have some of the lowest levels of violence in the world. And even in places that are modernizing, you're seeing the tide turn against violence. India, for example, is finally starting to protect women and girls from violence."

Quinn nods again. "Fair enough. What is leading this trend?"

"Secularization," Abby offers. "Places that see decreased religious intensity typically see a corresponding drop in violence."

"Right, Ms. Hilliard. So if secularization is leading to reduced violence—Yes, Mr. Douglas?"

"Sir, I don't think we can accept that secularization is leading to reduced violence because I don't believe we're actually seeing a reduction in violence. The author bracketed the wars in Iraq and Afghanistan, basically pulling them out of his sample to make his argument. The end of the Cold War has made the world less safe, not more."

"Why do you say that, Mr. Douglas?" Quinn sounds interested, not offended, which I'm taking as a good thing.

Except that now I have to keep going. And sooner or later, this conversation will derail into something personal. Something that pushes at the edges of my control. Guess I should have quit while I was ahead.

Abby

Josh is engaged, and it is a sight to behold. Fired up and participating in the discussion in a way that's not threatening to Professor Quinn. Which is good. Very good.

The tension in him from that first class isn't there, or if it is, he's transformed it into something else. Something...he can use.

"The war in Iraq. The fall of the Iraqi government. The collapse of Syria. We don't even know the full weight of the casualties from these conflicts," Josh says. "But I can also tell you that violence has definitely not decreased. The fall of Saddam allowed old scores to be settled, and believe me, they were settled. Violently. The author doesn't get to throw the last fifteen years or so out because they don't support his argument."

"So your argument is that the wars in Iraq and Afghanistan are evidence of more violence, not less; is that correct?" Professor Quinn remarks.

"Yes, sir."

Parker's hand shoots up. "These are religious conflicts," she says. "If we continue to advance education initiatives around the world, we can continue the gains that the introduction of reason has had on the advancement of civilization." She shifts and looks like she's enjoying herself tremendously.

I raise my hand. "There's no evidence that religion is actually on the decline. It's growing rapidly even in places where it's supposedly gasped its last. In Europe, more people are identifying as religious—just not Christian. In South America, the fastest growing religion is Pentecostal. And religious people have more babies, so even if we accept the premise that religion is declining in the current generation, there's no guarantee that it will continue to decline once the children of religious individuals grow up and take their place in the adult world."

Quinn holds up both hands. "Okay, so clearly we have some impassioned opinions on each side. One side suggests that violence is declining. The other says that it's an illusion. So why does it matter?"

It's a simple question, but beside me, Josh tenses.

"What?" I whisper.

He shakes his head, looking down at his hands. His knuckles are white on the pencil.

"War," he says softly.

Quinn looks up at him. "A little louder, Mr. Douglas?"

"War. If violence is actually declining, it takes away the need for war. It makes war unnecessary."

"Well, then the military would be out of a job." Parker smirks over at him, and I instantly want to throttle her. "And war is never necessary."

Josh twists the pen violently between his fingers. "I don't think that war will ever become obsolete. There are some who will not be reasoned with."

Parker shakes her head. "You're not going to argue about the power of belief again, are you?"

He swallows hard, his fingers twisting that pen like he's going to snap it in half. "I wouldn't underestimate it. How else can you explain mothers willingly sending their children to be suicide bombers?"

"Mental illness." Parker shrugs. "Clearly, only someone who is clinically insane would send their child off to die. It's contrary to what we know about human nature. We are fundamentally selfish, and we are trying to pass our genes along to the next generation. Killing them doesn't make any sense."

"I have to agree with Parker." I shoot Josh an apologetic glance. "It doesn't make any sense. Humans are selfish."

Josh shakes his head. "I disagree. He has no

greater love than he who would give his life for another."

"You're quoting a religious text to make your argument?" Parker asks, and her words are laced with skepticism and a barely concealed sneer.

But Josh doesn't back down in the face of her contempt. "If we accept that there are some fundamentals about human nature buried in religious texts, then yes, a religious statement makes my argument. We're not selfish—not like rational choice theory would have us believe."

"If we're not selfish, what are we?" Professor Quinn asks. "And what does this have to do with violence?"

Josh is practically vibrating now. His back is tight, the muscles in his neck bunched and tense. "We're social, sir. And that means I will gladly lay down my life so that my brothers can come home, even though we share not one drop of the same blood."

A slow smile spreads across Quinn's face. "Mr. Douglas raises the fundamental problem of violence—how does it enable social cohesion while at the same time being so destructive?"

Parker's hand shoots up. "Wait a sec. Is violence declining or not?"

Quinn clicks on a slide that shows a single graph with a massive spike in it toward the right side. "From the data that we have—and mind you the data is actually quite terrible—what we see is that violence tends to hover around this trend line. But periodically, there are spikes. The last great spikes were World Wars I and II. This suggests that violence is neither increasing nor decreasing, but rather is merely returning to its normal levels after a massive global conflict."

I frown, thoroughly confused by the entire discussion. "What are we supposed to take away from this?"

Quinn flips to an image of a mushroom cloud over an island. "This class is centered on violence. But violence and religion are intertwined, it seems, so we cannot have a discussion about one without the other. It's easy to accept the argument the author makes that violence is declining because we want to accept it. But if religion is merely lying dormant—and all demographic information seems to suggest that this may be only a passing trend, then it means we should expect to see a greater resurgence of religion, not a decrease."

"Which means a resurgence in violence," Josh says quietly. "More war."

Parker shakes her head and shoots her hand into the air. "Sir, I have to disagree. The current generation is the least religious in history. They do not identify as religious. How will their children take up this belief system if it's not taught to them at a young age?"

Just like that, the light bulb goes off. "It makes perfect sense. How many kids are you going to have?" I ask Parker.

Parker shrinks from the question. Just a little but

it's enough that I notice. I didn't mean to strike a nerve, but clearly I did.

"Right. And how much of the American population is in college right now?"

She shrugs. "I don't know. Half?"

"Less than a third," I tell her. "Which means that all those people out there not going to college are likely having babies. If even half of their babies are religious, it's more than any of your babies because you didn't have any. Religious people and less educated people have more babies. Which means that when their kids grow up, there's a strong likelihood that they will be religious or uneducated just like their parents because we know that parental religiosity influences their children's."

I'm trying to focus on Parker, but it's Josh who is claiming my attention. The discussion is about violence, but damn if I don't feel actual violence radiating off him in pulsating waves.

I touch his shoulder as the focus of the discussion shifts away from Josh and me. "What's wrong?"

He shakes his head once, and I let him be. Now is not the time. But something about this conversation set him off.

A cold worry slides down my spine to wrap around my belly.

Chapter Thirteen

Josh

Class couldn't end soon enough. It should have been an interesting discussion. Violence and belief discussed in cool, academic terms. Emotionless. Rational.

And yet, it was exactly that cold, academic level of the discussion that set me off.

Violence isn't cold. It's not rational.

It is hot. Burning. Thrashing. Tearing at everything and everyone around it until there is nothing left. It is not helpless. It is not passive.

It is action. It is motion and energy.

It is alive, a force of its own.

It's one thing to discuss it in class. It's another to have lived it. To have squeezed the trigger of your weapon and know that another's life has ended directly because of your actions. And that if you do not act, then someone you care about will die.

It sounds so simple in class. Away from the violence and the chaos.

But it's not. And the legacy of it is twisted and complicated, and I'm afraid it will never, ever let me go.

I have to fight this. I want to come home.

I want a chance. A chance with Abby.

I want to be with her. I want to take her back to my place where it's quiet and dark and try to forget about the war and what it's done to me.

But it's robbed me even of that. The simple pleasure of lying skin to skin has been stolen from me.

"What happened back there?" she says, falling into step with me. We walk out of the old gothic building and into the construction zone of central campus.

I shrug, not sure how to answer. It's a long moment before I respond, wondering how much of the reality she's willing to absorb. "It's just hard to talk about violence like you're getting a tooth pulled, you know?"

A simple, uncomplicated version of the truth.

Her hand is warm on my shoulder, and I want to pull her against me. To bury my face in her neck and breathe her in.

"I get that," she says quietly.

I look at her, watching her silently. "I hope not."

Her smile is flat, her vibrant golden eyes sad. "We all have stuff in our pasts we're trying to outrun."

There is more she's not saying. A sadness in her eyes that makes me want to ask her what she knows about violence. A fear in my own heart that her answer will not be "nothing".

I don't want to think of her hurting.

But now isn't the time. I suppose it never is.

"Not Parker." I deliberately try to shift the conversation.

Her eyes sparkle brightly. "Even Parker," she says.

Her arm brushes against mine, and I seize the moment to thread my fingers with hers.

"Who hurt you?"

Her fingers spasm. "Let's just say Mom didn't make good choices after my dad died."

I take a step closer and cup her face with one hand. She practically purrs against my touch. Something opens inside me, like a live thing reaching for the sun after a long winter's sleep. "I'm sorry for your pain," I whisper. "But without it, you wouldn't be who you are today."

She presses her lips together and looks away. "I think I'd be okay with that."

The world passes by around us. There is only Abby. The sadness in her eyes. The painful truth that both of us are more damaged than either one realizes.

"Don't say that." I lean closer, the need to taste her overpowering any notion of common sense. "I like you the way you are."

Her lips part beneath mine, a quick huff of breath a moment before I claim her. Slowly, her lips part and I capture her tongue, sucking gently, so gently. Her gasp is a thing of beauty, hitting me square in the chest and pulling me under in a wave of pleasure that is more potent than the strongest drug.

Making me want.

It takes everything I am to ease back, to put space between us. Her fingers flex on my sides. I want more. I want the rest of the afternoon to just explore her mouth with soft kisses and gentle strokes.

"What do you have next?" I ask. I'm amazed my voice is even working.

She takes a single step back. The distance might as well be a mile. "Work. Some alumni function, so I'm working an extra shift."

Slowly, she shifts back into the Abby I know from class. Polished. Professional. No hint of the passion in her touch. I've been given a hint of a secret thing. And it is not enough. "Do you ever have any problems at those things?"

She offers a wry smile. "Is 'problems' a euphemism for drunk groping?"

See? I told you she was perceptive. "Maybe."

She shrugs. "Not really. Most of the time people behave."

I swallow and grip her fingers a little tighter. "Would I be setting feminism back a century if I admit that I'm uncomfortable with the idea that you've had to fend for yourself?"

We turn down a wooded path toward the country club that rests just off main campus. People don't often associate country clubs with college campuses but this one has been here since the university's first building was erected. Old money and all that.

She surprises me when she stops in front of me

and slides her arms around my neck. I rest my fingertips along her sides, wanting more. I want to back her up against the hundred-year-old oak tree and lift her legs around my waist. I want to kiss her for hours and hours. I want. And I know I can't. She's going to work. She can't show up with tree bark in her hair at a place where they serve twenty-five-dollar martinis and hundred-dollar scotch.

She presses against me, her body soft and strong and infinitely feminine. "It's probably setting feminism back a hundred years if I admit that hearing you go all caveman protective does something funny to my insides."

A bolt of heat spikes down my spine and tightens in the vicinity of my balls. The sharp, sudden pleasure is unexpected and oh so welcome. It's the closest thing to arousal I've felt since before things went to hell in my life.

"You're trying to kill me, aren't you?" I whisper near her ear.

"Maybe." She makes a warm sound. "Maybe it's been a long time since I felt like this with anyone."

I tug her close and breathe in the scent of her, clinging to the normalcy of the moment. Wishing it would last forever. Knowing that it won't.

"Can I walk you home tonight?" I ask. I brace for her to say no again.

She brushes her thumb across my bottom lip. "I'd like that very much."

I don't want this time to end. I'm like a starving man, dying and hungry for her. Just her and the way

I feel when I'm around her.

And I let her go. Because I have to remember how to live without her.

Abby

I'm supposed to be doing my homework. I'm on a break at the Baywater and I'm trying desperately to focus on my assignment for Quinn's class.

This week's readings are quite literally hitting too close to home.

It's a section on domestic abuse.

And holy shit it is hard to read.

"You look like you're reading an obituary. Did someone die?"

I look up at Graham as he walks into the break room, then do a double-take when the joking tone of his voice stands in stark contrast to the damage on his face.

His left eye is swollen and purple. There's a small cut on his cheek. And his eyes, normally smiling and laughing, are bleak and filled with sadness.

I'm on my feet, assignment forgotten. "What happened?"

He shrugs and offers a sad smile. "Walked into a door."

My skin goes cold. My dinner turns into a solid ball in my stomach. I want to make a joke. I want him to laugh and tell me it's not what I think.

I cannot stand there and look at one of my best friends with a black eye and not think the worst.

Please don't say anything, Abby. It'll just make it worse.

I am eleven years old again. I am standing helpless in the kitchen where my mother is holding a frozen bag of blueberries wrapped in a towel to her split and bleeding lip.

My mouth moves, but no sound comes out. I can't form a coherent thought.

"My resident makeup artist friend is out of town for a fashion show or I would have asked him for help hiding the bruise." His voice breaks, and with it, my control.

I wrap my arms around his waist and just hold him. He's stiff for a moment, then relaxes into my embrace. Graham has been a rock for me and it breaks me a little bit to see him hurting like this.

A shudder runs through him. I blink rapidly, trying so hard not to fucking cry.

"Men really suck sometimes," I whisper.

He makes a strangled sound and straightens, stepping back out of my arms. "Don't I just know it."

"The boss isn't going to be happy with you behind the bar with a shiner." I take his hand. "Come on. Let's see if the apprentice has become a master."

It feels like a lifetime ago when Graham took me under his wing. He had Mitchell, his friend who did makeup at the local department store, show me how to do my own makeup so that I looked polished and posh. Over the years, I've passed that skillset on to new friends who arrived here, looking out of place.

Passing comes in all forms. And those of us who are first generation have a better chance of making it if we stick together.

Graham sits at the small table. I try to move my book before he sees it but I'm not quick enough. The silence is so strange without him making a joke or some sarcastic comment. "How's that for ironic? A college course on violence." He looks over at me. "Bet there's not much about the gay community, is there?"

I shake my head as I start laying out the supplies I'll need to conceal the bruising. "It remains very much a woman's issue."

Which sucks because real people get hurt when we pretend that the issues simply don't exist in other communities. "Want to talk about it?" I carefully apply green tinted primer to his skin, patting as gently as I can to avoid causing him any more pain.

I hate this. I hate the bruise on his skin. I hate the dark stain beneath his eyes and the red rimming them.

I hate the pain that love causes.

I stop myself. It's not love that does this. It's never love.

This is hate. And it uses love, twisting it and drawing it close until it can destroy it or turn it into something unrecognizable.

He winces and I pause, giving him time to pull everything back in. "Turns out Mr. Wonderful isn't a vegan body builder after all. He's been juicing the whole time and I don't mean carrots." Graham winces as I pat the first layer of concealer in place. "I caught him and called him on it. You don't really need the details. Just pull up every stereotype about 'roid rage you can think of."

I hold up a couple of different pots of concealer to his face, hoping that I've got one that'll be close to his skin tone.

"Guess I'm lucky you have an inner RuPaul and not an inner Martha Stewart, huh?"

I choke on the strangled laugh and lower my forehead to his. "That's not even funny." But I'm smiling through tears as I start patting concealer into place with a brush, being as gentle as I can. I will not fall apart on him. He needs me to keep my shit together. And that's exactly what I will do. "Are you going to report him?"

He shakes his head. "Do you know what happens when a gay man walks into a police station to report domestic abuse?"

I make a noise. "It's probably on par with what happens when a girl from the wrong side of the tracks tries, huh?"

"Probably. You get all of the 'what did you do to deserve it?' I get 'that's what you get for sucking cock.' And you don't have to say it. I know it's not all cops." He presses his lips together and blinks rapidly.

"Don't cry. You'll ruin your foundation."

He laughs quietly. "That was my biggest fear."

I set the concealer with a translucent powder

then hand him a mirror. "I'm not as talented as Mitchell but I think it'll get you through the night without our boss freaking out."

He turns his head and inspects my work. "Very nice. Now I don't have to use it as small talk behind the bar." He tugs me down on the small chair next to him. "Thanks, hon."

"For doing your makeup?"

"For not pushing me to report him. For just listening."

I rest my head against his shoulder for a moment. "That's what we do, right? We stick." I shift and look up at him. "Want me to go with you when you get your stuff out of his place?"

He smiles. "While I realize you are a badass, I'm not sure you're going to intimidate all two hundred and fifty pounds of not vegan body builder."

"No but I could at least hope that he'll behave in front of company." I squeeze his hand. "I don't think you should go back alone, that's all."

"You're probably right but shouldn't you be making plans with Sergeant Sexy Pants?"

Graham is entirely too perceptive. "When did he stop being Mr. Tall, Dark, and Depressed and start being Sergeant Sexy Pants?"

I want to tell him how, for the first time in my life, a man didn't make me feel bad for being who I was.

"Nice dodge." I look over at him. "You don't get to say no. I'm not letting you do this alone."

He squeezes my hand. "Maybe I'll go back tomorrow or something. Not tonight."

I nod and we both head out to work. I smile and nod and make all the right noises.

But I am pulled away. I can't think, can't focus.

And when the alumni event ends an hour early, I clock out. Escaping the polish and glossy life at the Baywater for something else.

Something real.

And I only hope I can find it.

Chapter Fourteen

Josh

There is still an hour before I'm supposed to meet Abby. I take a long pull off my beer, wishing the time would hurry the hell up already. Caleb is at the end of the bar, talking with a girl who clearly looks like she'd believe him if he told her he was a Nazi hunter.

"Doesn't he have some hapless girlfriend, or is every female of the species at risk?" I ask Eli, only mildly curious why he's on the prowl tonight.

"Apparently she caught his dick playing hide-and-seek somewhere it wasn't supposed to be and she dumped him," Eli says quietly.

I raise my glass in mock salute to her. "Guess she's smarter than I gave her credit for." Anyone with a brain in their head isn't going to be able to stand being around Caleb for more than ten minutes.

I glance down the bar. Caleb is leaning a little too close to the girl. There is a comfort in his every move. A confidence.

"He fits right in here, doesn't he?"

Eli shakes his head, his eyes dark. "He's got just as much a place here as you."

I tip my glass. "Sure enough."

Eli opened this bar specifically to draw in local veterans and apparently, he's got a knack for finding the walking wounded and bringing them into the fold. I admire him for what he does. I couldn't do it, but he's right in more ways than one. We need each other—we're the only people who get what our brothers and sisters in arms have gone through.

Guys like Caleb don't need people like me. He's an officer, a West Pointer. Caleb fits here among the rich kids and the big brains. But even with all that, I can't for the life of me figure out why Eli scooped him up. He reeks of old money and East Coast elitism.

I sigh over my beer. I really don't feel like fucking dealing with everything about Caleb that drives me over the cliff of sanity. He hasn't seen me yet, which is a good thing. I'm going to finish my beer and get the hell out of here.

"Fine. But it's on you if he triggers my PTSD by talking about how hard summer camp was at West Point." A joke is easier than the truth.

And the truth right now isn't something I can risk unpacking. Not without bringing up some really bad memories.

Eli grins and it's amazing how not scary he looks when he smiles.

Then again, going to war changes a guy. I've never seen what he looked like before the war. I suppose going to war counts as a transformative event. I'm damn sure not the person I was before I left.

Just like that, old pain resurrects, and I take another long pull off my beer, trying to find something to anchor me to the world before I slip into an alcohol-induced abyss.

I deliberately circle my thoughts back to Abby and meeting her in an hour. I glance at my watch. Fifty-three minutes. I haven't seen her since that moment after class, but I haven't been able to stop thinking about her. It was the closest thing to aroused I'd felt in as long as I could remember. I'm twenty-five years old. I'm not supposed to be celibate, but the fucking war has neutered me.

The door to the bar swings open, and I see her the moment she steps into the dark interior.

Something is wrong. I was supposed to meet her. And yet, she's here. One look at her face and I'm on my feet, crossing the space to her. "What is it?"

I want to put my arm around her. I want to pull her close and let her lean before she collapses. "Can we go somewhere?" Her voice breaks, shattering my heart with it.

"Yeah. Sure. Let me close out my tab with Eli."

I step back to the bar and hand Eli my card. Caleb stumbles back to the bar from the latrine. His Brooks Brothers shirt is untucked and wrinkled and he smells like he crawled out of a bottle of tequila. He slaps me hard on the back.

I barely manage to keep my expression neutral even as I shift to keep him away from Abby. There's something about the way he looks at women that's…unsettling. I'm trying to behave, if only because Eli asked me to and because Abby is here.

I'd really like to avoid her seeing the worst of me at the moment.

I just want to get out of here, away from him and the thousand bad memories he's resurrecting just by breathing. I might completely lose my shit if he starts in about what a badass he is.

Hatred is a powerful thing and Caleb—not the person but what he represents—is on the short list.

Jesus, Eli needs to close my tab out so I can get the hell out of here.

"Hey, look at you." Caleb glances over at Abby and nudges me in the elbow. "Finally gonna get some, huh?"

Just like that, Caleb crosses the line. It's an innocuous statement, one that shouldn't set me off. But I know this guy and I know where his mind just went, taking Abby with him into the filth and the grime and the grit. My hand moves before my brain fully engages and I shove him back. "Watch your mouth."

He smiles and it is cold and patronizing. "No need to be so fucking sensitive. She's just a piece of ass."

I react before I really think.

I slam my fist into his face. His cheek splits open and the sight of his blood feeds the need in me for violence. To hurt him for those hateful words. I hope to Christ Abby didn't hear him.

The blow sends him sprawling across the barroom floor, and I'm about to follow him down, but Eli is there, blocking me from taking his fucking head off.

I shake my hand and take a step away from Caleb, who has managed to push himself upright. Blood splatters on his pale blue Brooks Brothers button-down.

Hitting him felt better than it should have.

Eli steps between me and Caleb and jabs his finger toward the door. "Out."

I guide Abby out of the bar, unsure of where to put my hands, what to do with them.

"Friend of yours?" she asks. There's forced lightness in her voice, a tension that mixes with whatever was there when she came into the bar.

I need something to fill the void between us. Something to distract me from the look in Caleb's eyes that filled me with disgust. Maybe I was just looking for a fight.

I was, but that doesn't mean Caleb doesn't need his ass whipped. Just thinking about it gets my blood burning again.

"Not exactly." I drag my hand through my hair and breathe slow and deep.

"Looks like there's a history there." Her voice is quiet. Husky and thick and reserved.

"He's…he reminds me too much of my old platoon leader."

"Sounds like you miss the guy."

Her comment catches me off guard and I smile

unexpectedly. "Something like that."

"Do you miss it? The Army?"

I swallow at the innocence in that question. How can you miss something that destroyed you? That would have taken everything you had? "Yeah, I guess I do."

"What do you miss?"

"Everything. The guys. The stupid shit my soldiers used to do." I hesitate. "The sense of purpose, I guess. That what I did mattered."

She stops then and her fingers find mine. She cups my face with her free hand, her touch soft and oh so compelling. "What you do matters, Josh," she whispers. A moment before she kisses me.

There is darkness in that kiss. A reaching out, grasping for something to hold on to. I'm pulled under, needing, hoping.

The drinking, the emotional distance—I feel a deep sense of shame because those things extend from my time in the Army. And I'd give anything to be back there now in the stink and the heat and the chaos.

I'm supposed to be an educated man; I'm supposed to know better than to bury my emotions in a drink or six, lamenting the loss of purpose in my life.

Until I met Abby, I was content to burn away the best years of my life missing the worst years of it. Now? Now I am being drawn slowly toward the light, after being in a pool of darkness for far too long. There is a faint stirring of arousal that is so much more than a fleeting sensation of an erection.

It's hope.

Hope that maybe what ails me is only temporary. That maybe, just maybe, I'm not forever fucked up from the war.

That maybe someday I can put the pieces of my broken life back together because I'll have something or someone else that makes me feel like a man again.

But until that day comes, I'm stuck. In the shadows. Wanting, wishing, hoping for a chance to step back into the light.

Abby

There is too much churning inside Josh—inside me—and I'm not sure I can handle him falling apart if I'm already so close to the edge myself. I needed an excuse to touch him, to lose myself in his taste, his touch.

I need to escape. Before everything comes spilling out and Josh looks at me like I'm damaged and unworthy and unlovable. I'm not sure what it would do to me if he ever looked at me like Robert did.

It might break me.

"I needed that," I say quietly against his mouth when I can breathe again.

"Yeah?" He strokes his thumb over my cheek. The roughness of his touch is a balm, calming and exciting all at once. "What happened?"

"Friend of mine was slapped around by his boyfriend," I admit after a moment.

"Graham?"

I frown, unable to look away from the genuine concern in his eyes.

"You know him?"

"We chatted at the Baywater."

"No smartass comments?"

"You keep being surprised by the fact that I'm not some mouth-breathing Neanderthal."

"Well, the Army isn't exactly known for being a bastion of tolerance."

"Maybe before the war. Now all we really care about is whether you can do your job. Gay, black or otherwise, most people don't give a shit. Will you do what it takes to get everyone home? That's the stuff that matters."

There's a roughness in his voice. There's more to that story.

"You're not going to ask?" he says after a moment.

I shrug, grateful for the distraction from my own worries. It's so much easier to focus on someone else's. "Do you want to talk about it?"

"Not particularly." There is something dark there, simmering just below the surface. Ready to break free at the slightest provocation.

"Then I won't ask."

He makes a noise. "You're pretty uncurious for a girl."

I tuck my hands into my jacket pocket and we

start walking again. "I guess I understand not wanting to talk about everything with everyone." I look over at him. "People aren't entitled to having their curiosity satisfied."

That noise again. I can't decide what that means.

But I don't ask. For now, I'm content to be with him. To be facing down at least one shadow of the nightmares that haunt my life.

He glances over at me, and I can physically feel the half-truth standing between us. "Why did you come to The Pint tonight? I would have met you at work."

I shrug again. I'm not being deliberately coy. I just can't find the words to tell him how much it hurts seeing Graham in pain. "Maybe I just didn't want to be alone."

He stops walking. He slides his hands over my shoulders and turns me to face him. His palm is warm on my cheek, his thumb slipping over my skin. His face is cast in shadows from the streetlamps overhead.

He's calm now; the violence in him either contained or dissipated. Not gone for good, though. I've seen this kind of violence before and it's never really gone. There's a storm brewing in the distance. Thunder rumbles closer from the west.

"We're going to get rained on." My voice is thick. I wasn't lying. I don't want to be alone.

I'm tired of running from the memories of the past. Tired of pretending to have all my shit together. I want to ask him to take me someplace.

Tired of having to be strong for everyone around me. Tonight, just for tonight, I want to lean on someone else. Even if that leaning takes the form of something hot and mindless and slicked with sweat, it will allow me to pretend, if only for one moment, that I am just a regular person. That I don't have to be strong all the time.

I take a single step closer to him. The muscles in his throat move as he swallows. His lips part, his breath is warm on my skin. His fingers spasm against my cheek.

No, the violence in this man is not gone.

And I'm afraid. Not of him but of what he represents. I'm afraid of my reaction to this man, to the violence in his soul. Fear and arousal are twisted inside me. I want this.

I want to do this without shattering.

But it might break open all the old wounds before I'm able to handle them.

"I don't live far from here." His voice is harsh. Rough and strained.

Like the man. Caged and contained by a façade of modern life.

His thumb pauses against my cheek. His mouth is there, just there. A breath from mine. I am aching, hurting and needy all at once.

I close my eyes and lean in, resting my forehead against his. For a moment, the world falls away and it is just him and just me, and we are alone in the shadows and the light.

I'm terrified of taking this step. There's no going

back after this.

And I want this. I can handle this. If I keep telling myself it, it will be true.

"I would very much like to go home with you." The words do not get caught in my throat. They flow between us, carrying the invitation, the request from my lips to his.

A shudder runs through him. I can feel the vibration in the space that separates us.

"Abby."

Both hands are cradling my cheeks now. As though he was holding something fragile and worth more than a thousand suns.

But it's just me beneath his fingertips.

He says nothing more until I open my eyes. The storm is there, looking back at me. Watching. Waiting.

"Tell me what has you sad." Such a simple request. One that I think I love him for.

I slip from his touch and thread my fingers with his. I'm not sure how much I can talk about tonight. Not sure what I can resurrect without falling to pieces, something I'm trying desperately to avoid.

I take a deep breath and hold it until it burns.

When I finally speak, it's not what either of us is expecting. "I suppose you're used to being asked about war."

His fingers spasm against mine and it is a long moment before he answers. "Yeah." Another silence. "Though not as much here as you'd think. I thin…I think people here don't really want to know about it." He glances at me. "Or at least what they think they know about war."

I offer a half-hearted smile. "They're against it."

He makes a noise. "Right."

"There are a lot of assumptions about you. Because you're a veteran."

"I think I'm always one step away from becoming every stereotype they already think I am." He pauses. "I feel like every time I open my mouth, I risk finally meeting everyone's expectations. The angry veteran. Can't piss him off. PTSD might start acting up and he might snap and shoot the place up."

He's trying to be flippant but it fails beneath the weight of his bitterness. It surprises me, honestly, at the level of anger in those words.

"I get that," I finally tell him. "Not the angry veteran, but the expectations? I think it makes life just that much harder for me here because I'm always worrying how people will take what I say or do."

He holds the door open to his apartment building. It's an older brick building at the edge of campus. Not far from the bars and the old shops that were the first in the area to be gentrified.

I follow him silently down the worn carpet corridor to an old door that looks like it's been painted over a dozen times or more.

He pulls out his keys and opens it, letting me into his world, his life.

But I don't have time to take in his apartment.

As soon as the door closes behind us, he backs me slowly against it. I'm aware of his space at the periphery of my senses, but it is Josh who holds my attention.

His body is long and lean against mine, a solid wall of muscle that surrounds me. His mouth hovers just near mine. He does that a lot. This almost-but-not-quite-kissing thing.

It's driving me a little insane.

"You never struck me as worried about what people think." Soft words that are a balm on the ragged, exposed wounds I'm trying to bandage over once more.

"Maybe there's a lot you don't know about me." Sometimes, the truth is easier than a lie.

"What made you hurt tonight?" he whispers against my mouth.

"Maybe I'm trying not to think about it." I want to lose myself in his kiss, but he's holding himself apart. Just enough to make me contemplate serious bodily harm.

He makes a warm sound. "So you need a distraction?"

Oh sweet baby Jesus yes please.

But I can't talk. Because he covers my mouth with his and I am gone, sinking into the sensations he strokes to life inside me with each flick of his tongue.

Chapter Fifteen

Josh

She's not telling me the truth. At least not all of it. I haven't known her long but I know she's a pretty straight shooter. She is hurting tonight. I know this. I can see it as clearly as I've seen anything in my life.

And she came to me.

I slide my tongue against hers, needing, wanting to make her tremble. It's a need inside me, burning for her. Only her.

I want to take away the pain and make her forget her own name.

I cradle her face in my hands, kissing her deeply, tasting all of her. Her scent surrounds me, something warm and rich and smooth. She makes me forget. Makes me feel.

And feeling something other than dead inside is so fucking rare for me these days.

I slide one fingertip down the smooth line of her throat. Her pulse scatters a ragged beat beneath my touch and she makes a warm sound deep in her throat.

"I like that." A throaty whisper in the darkness.

"You have talented fingers."

I smile against her mouth. "I haven't even gotten started yet."

Her arms thread around my neck. "Yeah?" She nuzzles my throat, her breath hot on my skin. "What else do you have planned?"

I stiffen. I know she means it as a joke, but it hits me in the soft parts below the waist. I kiss her to hide my reaction because I have no fucking clue what I've gotten myself into.

I have no idea how to do this. How to fuck the woman in my arms senseless while hiding what the war has done to my body. To my fucking soul.

But there's no time like the present to figure it out.

Abby is here. In my apartment. And I am not going to waste this opportunity to love her like I've been dreaming to.

I lift her then, sliding her legs around my waist, never breaking the kiss, never losing the sweetness of her mouth on mine.

I make it all the way to my bedroom, glad that it is at least laundry day so everything is piled in one corner as opposed to scattered around my space like it normally is.

My relief is misplaced. I trip over a goddamned shoe and stumble to the bed, twisting just in time so that Abby falls on top of me.

"Wow, those are some impressive reflexes you've got there." She's smiling down at me but I'm borderline incoherent. She's straddling my hips, her body pressed to mine in all the right places.

Panic spikes through me that she'll figure out just how fucked up I really am. I pull her down, rolling until she is beneath me.

She is fire in my arms. Burning, liquid fire penetrates the dead zone inside of me.

I want to feel her body pressed against me. The warmth of her skin against mine. I crave her. She is more than a need to me.

She is hope.

And she has demons she's been hiding from the world. As confident as she comes off in class, I can't help but see the insecurity she tries to hide. As badly as I want to strip her naked and taste every inch of her body, I have to do this right.

I lean back then, tugging her with me until she's sitting up in my bed. I can smell myself on her and it hits me center mass with a sense of belonging. I want to see her in my clothes.

But not right now.

I swallow. My mouth is suddenly dry and I am very much not sure about how this whole thing is going to go down.

But it's better this way.

I watch her watching me slide the buttons of my shirt open. One by one.

I'm not exactly accomplishing the whole hiding thing but I don't have to get naked for her to see me. She'll probably figure things out before I'm ready to tell her anyway.

Her eyes darken as I drop my shirt to the floor.

Her eyes are drawn to the black ink etched into my skin. She is still, so still she might be a statue, frozen in ice. Her chest is barely moving as I lift the t-shirt over my head.

I'm not sure she's seeing me. Or if she's even in the room with me.

I don't know if it is something specific in the color splashed between the black lines, or if it's about the tattoos in general.

I stand there and let her be, let her absorb my own private hell drawn in full color over my body. It's been a few months since I had anything new done. My skin is healed, the ink immortalized in my flesh. For now. I'm drawn to the pain. It's like fighting. A delicious slide of a needle into your skin. It takes over every single thought until all you can feel, all you crave is the pain.

It's forever before she moves.

She crawls slowly into my space. The heat from her body warms my skin. I close my eyes. I want her fingers on me. I want her to touch the darkness and know that it's me beneath the violent ink spread across my body.

She circles behind me. I bow my head, knowing what she finds there.

The First Cavalry Division patch stretched across my back. The black horse head and the black slash across the bright yellow shield. And in that shield, the names of my brothers.

Each name. Permanently carved into living flesh.

"How many times did you go?"

"Twice." I can't open my eyes. "I wasn't there for the heavy fighting."

Then I feel it. The gentle trace of her finger down the center line of my spine. I shiver at the unexpected, erotic sensation.

But I am completely undone by what she does next.

Abby

I wrap my arms around his waist and rest my cheek against his shoulders.

I can hear my mother's cries. See the flashes of black and blue ink from the cut-rate tattoos when her boyfriend slaps her, shouting at her that she should control me. That she shouldn't put up with my mouth, my attitude.

I don't want to remember, but the memories are coming, rising up in the darkness. I feel ill, physically sick.

But I stay. I refuse to let the bastard who hurt my mother because of me rule my life any more. He's done enough damage. To me. To my relationship with my mother.

And I need to move on. I am so tired of being stuck in the past.

"What do you see when you see my tattoos?" A deceptively quiet, gentle question.

"My mom. Her boyfriend." I suck in a shuddering

breath. No sense in hiding it. It'll be harder later.

Josh is tense beneath my touch now.

"I see everything I lost when my dad died."

"He hurt you." A vibration of potential violence in his stillness.

"He hated me. Hated that I was mouthy. Hated that I talked back. He tried to tell my mom that I needed my ass beaten to learn some respect."

I force myself to look at the tattoo on Josh's back. I trace the outline of the guitar pick shape on his skin. He trembles beneath my touch. It unnerves me how such a simple reaction can send such a surge of pleasure bolting through me.

A pleasure laced with something forbidden.

I trace the edges of the black lines between his shoulder blades with the edge of my nail, then I press my lips to the center of his back. He sucks in a hard breath and makes a strangled noise deep in his chest. The sound vibrates through his body and into me.

"When he couldn't get his hands on me, he punished her."

I stay there, frozen, long after those words, encased in years' worth of shame, have left my lips and tainted the air around us.

It's a long moment before Josh turns and draws me into his arms. He leans back, dragging me down with him into the tangle of sheets that smell warm and familiar. He kisses me, and it is soft and sweet and everything I never expected from anyone.

He is violence, caged and restrained. But at that

moment, he is the most thoughtful lover I've ever had. His mouth is gentle on mine, stroking, sipping, tasting. He cups my face. "He can't hurt you anymore."

"She's still with him." And I almost choke on the unexpected bitterness in those words. I thought I'd made peace with all of that.

Guess not.

"Christ, Abby, I'm sorry." He pulls me close, and I wrap my arms around him, surprised by how much those simple words hurt. It is an acknowledgment that everything I've tried to become has been built on a lie.

A charade.

I push out of his arms and lean over him, cupping his face with one hand. "Thank you."

He frowns. "For what?"

"For not judging me." I brush my lips against his.

"For what? Surviving a shitty childhood? That's easy." He grins against my mouth. "If you had told me you hate puppies or something, I might have had a hard time handling that."

He tangles his fingers against my hair and pulls me down, claiming my mouth. There is raw possession in this kiss and I am not for a moment fooled by his teasing words.

But I'm soon beyond thought as he kisses me and takes me out of this world to a place where there is only him and only me and the pleasure he strokes to life in my body.

It's one of the things I'm starting to love about

him. The strange paradox of this man. He wears ink carved into his skin beneath his t-shirts yet can argue philosophical and political theory like a man raised in expensive boarding schools. But when he touches me, he is just Josh. Pure. Simple. Energy and heat. As passionate in love as he is in everything.

I close my eyes as he peels the clothing from my body. Lose myself in sensation as he traces my breasts with his tongue. His touch is sensual and slow. Patient. Pressure and heat build inside me. I want his clothes off. I want to be skin to skin with him. Touching him like he's touching me. Exploring. Learning.

There is something freeing about giving myself permission tonight. To touch. To feel. To let go for once in my life.

His fingers are sliding over my skin. Slowly, lower. Lower. A caress of skin against my hip bone. And then his fingers slide beneath my panties and I am lost in a brilliant starburst of sensation as he strokes me where I am soft and wet and burning for him.

His lips follow his touch. He licks me, then blows on my skin. Warm and wet, hot and cold. I am nothing but a twisting mix of sensations.

I am not prepared for his mouth to press to my core, where I am wet and swollen.

I bolt upright off the bed, scooting my hips back, but he captures me. His smile is dark and wicked. The smile of raw masculine pride that shifts abruptly to confusion. His thumb strokes my inner thigh. He is patient. Waiting. Watching. "I thought most women liked that sort of thing."

I don't have the words to tell him that no one has ever done that to me before. I've never trusted anyone to…do that. It's too exposed. Too open. But I don't have the words I need to explain it. The words to make it not sound pathetic and insecure. It's something I've read about in novels but never experienced and now that I have, it is shocking in its intimacy.

But I can't say that because my throat is blocked off and my eyes burn.

If he notices, he doesn't say anything. Instead, he crawls slowly up my body until I can see only him, blocking out everything.

"Trust me?" He brushes his lips against mine and I can taste the lingering warmth from my body on his mouth.

It's kind of scary how he can read my mind. But I'm not questioning it. It's an escape. Words I don't need to find.

I make a rough sound in my throat as his fingers find my heat once more. He slides my panties to one side, kissing my throat. My chest. Inching his way down my body as I grow more and more tense with each slide of his fingers through my sex.

He makes a warm sound as he nuzzles me where I am exposed and vulnerable and aching. "Beautiful," he whispers.

And when he touches his tongue to me, I forget my own name, forget everything but the touch of this man that rocks my world.

Josh

I've found heaven. I'm a shitty poet but watching Abby surge off my bed when I barely touched her sent a spike of raw male power through my veins. I've been around the block a time or two but I've never seen anyone respond like she just did.

I slide my tongue over her clit again, gently, and her hips jerk in response. Pleasure, hot and thick, washes over me. Watching her, seeing her body respond—I've never been so fucking turned on in my life. My entire body hums with awareness as I taste her, making little designs with my tongue and listening to her cries.

She's so fucking wet. I could lose myself in her, but I can't. This is about her. Not me and the fucked up shit keeping me from returning fully from the war. This is one hundred percent about Abby.

I slip one finger inside her, and she damn near bucks off the bed.

"Holy shit that feels good." A ragged cry. A sob. She's so fucking gorgeous. Her skin is flushed and damp as I continue. Touching. Teasing. Tasting.

There's something simple about going down on her. About using my mouth and my fingers to drive her wild. It's deeply fucking erotic knowing that I'm the first man to touch her here like this. A primitive need rises inside me, preening that she's mine, only mine. That she's responding to my touch—to me. Fucked up, broken me.

I slip another finger inside her and her cries are

stronger now. Her thighs clench against my shoulders. She's glorious, spread out on my bed, her body thrumming in pleasure with every stroke of my tongue. I want to make her come. I want to hear her scream.

Her body arches with each slide of my fingers. I slip my thumb down, stroking the sensitive skin just below my fingers.

She comes then in a sudden burst of tension, her body spasming around my fingers. Wetness floods against my tongue as I draw it out, strumming her body like a high-tension wire.

It is only after that I slide my fingers slowly from her body and crawl up to lie next to her. She burrows closer, one thigh sliding between mine, one arm around my waist.

She kisses my neck and makes a sleepy sound.

I can't help feeling really fucking pleased with myself even as disappointment tries to wrestle the fleeting pleasure stolen away from me.

I close my eyes and just let myself be. I'm there. And for once, I'm not sliding down a black hole of alcohol-induced darkness.

"That was…pretty amazing," she whispers after a long silence.

I kiss the top of her head. Her hair is soft and springy against my lips. I think I love her hair. It's wild and bold and daring—just like Abby.

I grin in the darkness. "You're welcome."

She slaps my chest even as she laughs. "You sound so pleased with yourself." She leans up. "But you didn't…"

"It's not about me right now." I lean up, cupping her face. "This was about you." I kiss her gently. "Distraction accomplished."

She kisses me, and I'm lost again in the moment. In the sensations that are all Abby. Part of me can't believe she's here. That she's actually in my bed.

That she doesn't know how fucked up things really are with me.

I'd say that's a victory any day of the week.

She looks down at me, her golden eyes heavy and dark. "Thank you. For everything tonight." She traces her fingernail over the black heart tattooed over my chest. It's shaped like the muscle and wrapped in a crown of thorns. I was feeling particularly morbid and dark when I had that one done. "I swore I'd never date a soldier."

"Because of your dad?"

She shakes her head. "Because of Ray. My mom's boyfriend."

The rage is back, slowly burning away the fleeting pleasure. I only speak when I'm sure I've got things under control. "Is he still active duty?"

"I don't know. And I don't want to know, honestly."

"What's his last name?"

She looks at me sharply. "Why?"

"Because if he's active duty, the Army can do something about it."

She shakes her head and cups my cheek, kissing me sadly. "She won't leave him. It doesn't matter what the Army does."

I exhale sharply and pull her down into my arms, tugging the comforter over both of us. I wish she wasn't telling the truth but I saw far too much of this kind of thing when I served.

And as much as I want to believe the Army would do something to him if they found out about it, I know just how little they really care about things like domestic abuse. If they needed him, the value he'd bring to the unit would outweigh any allegations of abuse.

I lay there in the dark, helpless and angry at the world, wishing there was some way to fix even a small part of it. For her, for me. Anything would be a welcome change over the stasis that my life is at that moment.

It's a long time before she shifts against me, her body arching into mine.

She's getting ready to go. I'm not ready for her to leave. I want to ask her to stay.

Please don't leave me.

But instead I kiss her gently. "I'll drive you home?"

"I'd like that."

I watch her dress, her body lithe and strong. She's a light in the darkness of my world.

And I will lose her the minute she finds out that I'm only half present in this world. The rest of me is still at war.

And always will be.

Chapter Sixteen

Abby

There you are."

I stop short, really not wanting to deal with the owner of that voice. I'm in a hurry to meet Josh at the library to go over our lecture notes from Quinn's class.

My ex may not be the dead last person on the planet I want to see, but he's up there in the running. Right next to the demon from The Exorcist and a few family members who can drop dead for all I care.

But because I'm trying to be polite in public and not be the stereotype people pretend they're not waiting for, I stop and turn. I leave one hand on the door. Just so he's clear that I am not planning on lingering in this conversation.

"Yes?" Yep, my tone is short. I can't summon the ability to care if he's calling me a bitch beneath his breath. If he hadn't been so insecure, he might not have been threatened by my refusal to sit in the corner like a good little trophy.

"Why aren't you returning my calls?"

"Maybe because I blocked your number months ago." I try, really try, to keep the sarcasm out of my voice.

He rubs the back of his neck and looks at me like he used to. Once upon a time, he would get me all twisted up inside with just a look. With his broad shoulders and wide smile, Robert is as close to being a god as a man can get. You wouldn't think he had a fragile male ego by looking at him.

"I wanted to see you."

"That's not really in the 'don't ever call me again' playbook," I say. I'm not interested in his concern, fake or otherwise.

Because he doesn't actually care about me. He cares about how I make him look, and I'm willing to bet money he's got some event that he wants me to attend with him to make people think he's a normal, well-adjusted, non-threatening black man in a wealthy, trying-to-pretend-it's-not-all-white business school. He stands in front of me, his arms over his chest, looking every bit the big, tough guy I fell for all those months ago.

Too bad it was all an act.

And I'm no one's trophy.

"We're not dating anymore. You made it abundantly clear that I didn't meet your expectations of a woman you can be seen with."

His jaw tightens. There he is. The insecure little man I know so well. "Maybe I was wrong. Maybe I…maybe I miss you being by my side."

I smile flatly. "You should have thought about

that before you asked me to shut up when that woman asked me why I didn't straighten my hair to make it look neater. It never occurred to you to speak up. To defend me so that I didn't have to be the angry black stereotype." I turn to go. Because the truth of it is, his silence hurt. I expect biting comments from strangers.

I also expect more from the people in my life.

I'm not sure why I am reacting this way. Maybe Robert's hand on my upper arm is the proverbial straw.

When his hand closes over my upper arm, I jerk away and slam my elbow into the glass door. Pain is a brilliant starburst up my arm as I nail my funny bone.

I swear. Loud enough that people inside the foyer pause and shift to get a better look at whatever they think is getting ready to happen.

I am so not doing this. Not here. Not ever.

"You don't have permission to touch me." My voice doesn't waver. Doesn't tremble. "Ever again. You made it abundantly clear where I stand with you, and I have more pride than to let someone try to change who I am." I'm not screaming. I'm not raising my voice. But damn it, he is going to get the point.

And maybe someday, I'll get him out of my head.

"Is everything okay?"

There is a part of me, a tiny part that I'm ashamed to admit exists, that wants to lean toward the strength and security I hear in Josh's voice. I can feel him like a solid wall behind me, and it takes everything I have not to let that relief show on my face.

I turn to him slowly and offer what I hope is a reassuring smile. "Sure. I was just coming to meet you."

I look back and see a hint of darkness that flashes in Robert's eyes. Just a moment and it's gone, but I remember the ugliness he hides beneath that smooth, collected exterior.

Josh is a solid wall between me and the freedom I need, but he is not watching me. He's staring at Robert. I've seen that look on his face before. Last night at The Pint, right before he knocked the guy at the bar on his ass. And as much as I might hate Robert, I don't want Josh fighting on campus.

"Are you okay?" It is only after he speaks that he looks away from Robert and down at me.

I reach out before I can stop myself. Maybe it's because I need the contact; maybe it's because I need the reminder that he is real and solid and good. I place my hand on his chest, right over the slow and steady beat of his heart. Those dark green eyes fill with an intensity that's as frightening as it is compelling.

"Let's go," I whisper when I'm sure I won't embarrass myself.

His gaze flicks over my shoulder then back down to me. The intent to harm is gone now, leaving only warmth in the darkness of his eyes. A warmth that draws me closer to this powerful, dangerous man when I know damn good and well I should be going in the opposite direction.

But still Josh doesn't move.

"You're shaking." His voice is low and deep, laced with worry that melts me a little more.

"I'm fine."

He swallows and I'm tempted, so tempted, to slide my fingers over the movement in his throat. To see if his pulse is racing like mine. To see how warm his skin would be beneath my touch.

He moves then, sliding his palm over my cheek. I want so badly to lean against his touch. Instead, I close my eyes and remain absolutely still. Afraid that if I move, a predator will rise behind his touch and chase me if I so much as flinch.

And I'm not so sure I wouldn't welcome the chase.

Josh

I'm marginally calmer now. And by marginally calmer, I'm no longer fighting the urge to go find the guy who was giving Abby shit and tear his spine out. Abby sits across from me in the carrel. We're alone, which is probably not where we need to be right now. At least, not me. With her. Damn it, I can't even think straight around her.

I'm staring at my hands, unable to look up at her. There is a shame choking me, thick and squeezing my throat. Shame at the intensity of my reaction. Shame that no matter how long and far away from the war I get, my first reaction is always violence.

Violence is easy. Violence is simple.

"You're angry." Her words are not a question.

"You're perceptive."

"And now you're cranky."

Her expression is tight and tense, despite her attempt at sarcasm. I smile thinly. "I'm worried."

She swallows and picks at her thumbnail. "That was Robert. He's my ex."

I figured as much. You don't get that fired up with someone who doesn't involve some broken emotional attachment.

But the thought of her with him does something to my insides. It hurts. Really hurts. And I can't explain why. I lock my fingers together, needing something to do with my hands. There is a need for violence in me right now. Not toward her. No, never that.

But there was something in her eyes when she'd been talking to him. Something that struck me forcibly as not Abby. Something that felt wrong.

"He knew how to hurt me. With words, not fists."

She'd been fighting something, standing there. I don't know what to do with the emotions rioting inside me. I'm not used to this. This feeling…it's a helplessness. And I don't have the words to explain.

"We were at an event one evening. Black tie affair at the Carlton Burke Hotel." She looks down at her hands and it takes everything that I am not to move.

To let her talk. "One of the bankers wives asked me why I didn't straighten my hair. To make it neater, she said." Her voice trembles a little. "I could have said nothing. I could have smiled and been polite and not caused any offense." I take a deep breath. "Robert politely told me to shut my mouth. That I was going to ruin everyone's good time simply by pointing out that I liked my hair the way it was." She swallows and finally looks up at me. "And that's why we're not together."

I take her hand in mine. "He was just like your mom's boyfriend then." I hesitate. "He couldn't take you the way you were."

She frowns, surprised by my answer. "Yeah, I guess he was."

Her fingers are soft and smooth as they slide over mine. They slip over my skin, and I am suddenly aware of my own roughness beneath her soft strength.

Her hands have been here, protected and safe in college. Turning the pages of books. Writing papers that were probably fucking brilliant. Mine have made war. Gripped the butt of a weapon. Wiped sweat and blood from my brothers' skin. They have made terrible decisions. Terrible, horrible decisions. Some that I regret. Others that I don't.

I can't tell her about that. I can't explain to her what walking in my nightmares feels like.

Or what it feels like to have killed and felt no remorse. Society tells us we're supposed to feel bad about killing. That it's something we're not supposed to do and if we do, we must regret it.

And therein lies the problem.

But seeing her with him—with Robert, because he has a name now—seeing what being around him did to the fierce, vibrant woman sitting across from me…it resurrects those instincts inside me. The need to protect. To shelter.

To be an unapologetic shield for her. "For the record, I like you just how you are."

"Josh." Her voice is a whisper. The slide of a single word through the silence.

I bite my lips together and look up at her. There, looking back at me, is the Abby I know. I turn my hand beneath hers until they are palm to palm.

"He hurt you." There is no question in my words.

"Not today," she whispers. There is a note of fear beneath her words and the violence inside me surges again—a caged, wild beast. I feel the rage rising inside me again. "But yes. In the past. That's a big part of why he's my ex."

"What else did he do?"

Her smile is tight now. She looks down at our hands. Her skin is dark against mine but in the low light of the carrel, our hands might as well be twin shadows in the dim light. "That, my friend, is a long story." She slides her index finger against the vulnerable skin of my wrist and the thin scar that circles the space. "Thank you for being there today," she whispers.

My fingers spasm beneath hers. I'm tempted to curl them around hers, threading them together, knitting her to me where I can hold her. Keep her safe from the bad things I know are out in the world.

From the hurt I saw in her eyes. I want her to trust me with that. The want hits me hard. I need to be honest with her. At least, as honest as I can be.

"I wanted to hurt him." I can't look at her. "I'm no stranger to violence," I say. She needs to know that. Right now, right up front.

Before I start to lay those feelings out before her and let her do with my heart what she will.

"I already figured that out," she whispers.

Silence stretches between us. Echoes of old memories.

"You're not going to ask about it?"

Her finger caresses the skin of my wrist, and in that gesture is a comfort that is an odd mix of erotic and comforting. I'm not sure how to react. Oh, I know how I want to react. But I won't do that. Not to her.

Her lips quirk into an odd smile. "I'm confident that you've been asked 'Is it like Call of Duty?' more than enough."

My smile matches hers now. "How'd you guess?"

"It's probably along the same amount of times I've been asked what it's like to live in the ghetto or what it's like to be in a drive by." There is dry resignation in her voice. The voice of someone tired of dealing with the same questions over and over again.

"That sucks." There's really no good answer to a comment like that. I can't pretend to know what it's like for her. No matter how much I'm convinced she belongs here when I don't, I'm sure walking in her shoes is an experience filled with uncertainty, always questioning when the next painful reminder that no, this isn't really our place will occur.

"You get used to it," she says. "But it doesn't mean I'm not conscious of doing the same thing to my friends." She shifts then and releases a quiet breath. "So I have to tell you something. And you might be upset with me." She slides her fingers from mine and opens her notebook. Instantly, I miss the contact.

She is still, avoiding my eyes. "I'm going with Graham tonight. To his ex's."

My first instinct is to say hell no. But it's not my call. And I can't take that away from her. "Am I allowed to not be happy about this?" I ask cautiously.

She smiles warmly. "Yes, you can be not happy."

"Can I ask why you have to go?" My hands are useless again. Helpless to protect those I care about.

"Because he's my best friend. And I don't want him to face this alone."

"Doesn't he have any big, bodybuilder friends? Maybe friends with dogs with bad attitudes and a penchant for testicles?"

She laughs. "The bodybuilder friend is the problem."

I drag my hand over my face. I want to beg her to let me go. Beg her to let me stand between her and her friend and the hurt they're potentially facing tonight. But I can't.

Because there is crushing impotence blocking my throat. "Shit."

I want. For the first time since coming home from the war, I want something other than to escape into Friday night fights at the bar.

And I have no idea what to do with the need rising inside me and drawing me slowly back toward the world of the living.

She slips from her chair into my lap, threading her arms around my neck. "Thank you," she whispers against my mouth.

"For what?" I nudge her lips with my own. I am starving for her. Her taste. Her touch. The feel of her breath mingling with mine.

"Not stopping me from doing this."

I lift both brows. "I didn't realize I have veto power." I tip my chin. "Do I?"

She smiles and it is warm and filled with a thousand unsaid things. "Not really. But it means a lot to me that you won't try to stop me from being there for Graham tonight."

I cup her cheek, craving the softness of her skin, drawing on the strength at the core of this beautiful woman. "I don't like it. But there is one thing I understand and that's the need to be there for the people that matter."

Because I can do nothing more, I kiss her. Offering her all the things I lack the strength to say.

Hoping that I can keep a lid on my fear. That I can keep it contained and keep it from ruining everything good that has slowly started building between us.

Chapter Seventeen

Abby

Are you sure you want to do this?"

Graham is fidgeting. And Graham isn't really a fidgeter by nature. He's a little manic sometimes, but he's never nervous and unsure of himself.

And right now, I feel nothing but angry at the man who did this to him.

"This is stupid," he says quietly. "I can replace everything I left there."

"I hear a 'but' in there." I'm nervous, but I won't let him see it. I'm here for moral support and I can't do that if I'm panicking. I won't screw this up.

He's been there for me since I got here. I'm not going to let him down.

"The only thing that matters is my dad's watch," Graham says. He glances over at me. "When I came out to my parents, I was so fucking scared. My mom…she refused to believe she didn't have something to do with it." He made a rude noise. "Like she somehow failed as a parent and made me gay."

"That's pretty shitty." There's no good response.

What can you say to someone when his parents have turned their backs on him?

"It would have been devastating if not for my dad. He just looked at me and said he didn't care so long as I was happy."

"Wow." I suddenly, bitterly, miss my own dad. I don't remember much of him, but part of me wants to believe he'd be the kind of man who would love me no matter who I brought home.

"I didn't have time to get it before I left after Todd hit me."

I squeeze his hand. "Then we're going to get it back."

He doesn't look so sure and honestly, neither am I. I don't have any idea how to do this.

I can't hear the sound of our feet on the floor over the pounding of my heart in my ears.

I am eleven years old and all I can see are the dirty combat boots at the edge of my vision. I am hiding in the dark once more, cowering and afraid of the violence that tried so hard to end me. All because I couldn't stop arguing with my mom about my hair.

Graham doesn't know. Otherwise, I'm certain he wouldn't have agreed to let me come with him.

But these are my issues, not his. And I am tired of letting my fear define me.

I thread my fingers with his as he knocks on the door. Muffled music ends abruptly.

I don't know what I was expecting, but Todd isn't really what I imagined. When Graham said vegan bodybuilding, somehow I had this image of an ugly, small man with too many food issues.

Instead, Todd is perfection. He's a beautiful man with perfectly toned arms and a jaw that could crack glass.

It's the beauty that hides violence.

Todd looks between Graham and me then focuses entirely on Graham. The bruise on Graham's face is still there. Less swollen and angry but still a mark on my friend.

"Really, Graham? You've got to come here with a girl? What kind of a man are you?"

Graham's shoulder brushes against mine. "I can tell you one thing I'm not," he says. "Yours."

I want to cheer. But I want to get away from the violence I see in Todd's eyes more.

Todd shifts tactics. It's a technique I've seen before so many damn times. Really, abusers need a better playbook.

"Would it matter if I said I was sorry?" Todd's voice is smooth silk, and I squeeze Graham's hand, letting him know I'm here for him.

"I can't have that conversation right now," Graham says.

It's so easy to say what you'd say if it were you. That you'd tell the man who hit you to burn in hell.

It's another thing entirely when you're standing next to your best friend and he has to confront his nightmare. He's not alone. For whatever it's worth, I'm with him. He doesn't have to face this alone.

And if that is the only thing I can do, then damn

it, this is what I will do.

"Can I get my things?" Graham asks.

Todd says nothing. He steps aside and holds the door.

A gentleman. Too bad he didn't remember these values before he put his hands on my friend.

I bite my tongue. I'm not here to run my mouth, no matter how much I want to tell this guy off. I'm moral support, and damn it, I'm going to be fucking moral.

God bless him, Graham is fast. He's back in what feels like a heartbeat. Maybe two.

"Guess you were serious about just getting the watch, huh?"

His smile is tight. I'm calm and collected on the outside. Inside, I'm a shaking, terrified eleven-year-old, wishing someone loved me enough to stand up for me.

But that never happens.

It doesn't stop the want. The hope for the fairy tale prince who loves me enough to help me slay my own dragons instead of expecting me to let him do the slaying.

It's a stupid fantasy.

Outside, the darkness feels comforting. A warm, safe space, free of flagrant violence.

"Are you okay?" Graham asks after a long silence.

"Shouldn't I be asking you that?" I look over at him.

He holds his hands up. They're shaking and his eyes are filled. His smile is tense. "I got the only thing I can't replace." He swallows and waits until I finally look up at him. "Thank you. For going with me. Having you there tonight kept this from turning into a shit show."

"It's part of the BFF handbook or something." I reach over and squeeze his shoulder. "I'm glad you got it back," I whisper.

He smiles sadly. "Me too."

A little piece of my world is okay. Graham is still hurting but he's safe.

And I didn't fall apart, didn't shatter.

I very much want to see Josh. I need to feel his hands on my body, feel his fingers slide over my skin. To wipe the memories away and replace them with new ones.

I cannot change the past.

But I don't have to live in it anymore.

Josh

I'm a little drunk. I didn't mean to get drunk but it was that or stare at my phone, sick with worry.

She texts me and tells me she's okay. I want to meet up with her. I want to see her. To confirm that yes, she is okay.

I don't, because I know she needed to do this. And I'm not going to let my own psychosis ruin something she needs to do herself. And a tiny sliver of shame slides over my spine. Of doubt that what we'd shared the other night was just a fleeting thing, a passing hookup destined for the memory banks to be recalled when I was too drunk or too fucking sad to avoid taking that stone from my ruck sack.

But I've reached the point of not knowing what else to do with myself. I can't sit at the bar any more.

I step out into the darkness.

And I am not so drunk that I miss Abby walking up, momentarily caught in the shadows cast between the overhead lights.

I see her.

She is beautiful. A soft mix of shadows and light. A beacon in the dark haze of alcohol and fatigue.

She doesn't turn away. Instead, she walks toward me. There is a hesitation in her movements.

"Hey." My best pick-up line.

"Hey."

"How did things go with Graham?" I honestly want to know.

"He got his dad's watch back."

There's something more, something she's not telling me. She's chewing on her inner lip, her hands stuffed in her pockets.

And just like that, the hypothetical violence we dissect in class is very real once more. "Is he okay?"

She tips her chin and looks at me, her golden eyes filled with sad questions. "You really are one of the good ones, aren't you?"

I pause, her question breaking through the haze in my brain, and I have to think hard on what I actually said, in case it was something deeply inappropriate. It takes me back a little, pushes behind a defense for a moment. To a place I'm not comfortable being pushed. "For asking if your friend is okay?"

She swallows and doesn't look away. It's one of the things that draws me to her. She went into a shitty situation tonight. For a friend. As a soldier, that kind of loyalty speaks to me, calls to me. Draws me closer to her.

As someone lost, looking to find his way home again.

Or maybe for the first time.

But she doesn't answer for a long time. "I'm sorry," she mumbles. "It's just you keep surprising me." I suddenly badly want to feel her lips on me. Her fingers. Her body pressed to mine.

The allure of that siren call is fierce and compelling.

Then her gaze collides with mine and she steps into my space.

I'm drunk. But not so drunk that I can't slip my hands around her waist and draw her closer. I resent the clothing between us, separating her skin from mine. I resent the streetlamp overhead, the city street that is not a private space.

"I'm a little drunk," I whisper against her mouth.

"I can taste that." Her words brush across my lips, followed by a fleeting sensation of her lips against mine. She is soft and sweet and tastes like mint and a thousand bright lights.

Her words send a cascade of imagery through my

brain, a starburst of her body spread beneath me, her dark skin cast in shadows and light. My mouth on her. Her taste on my tongue.

I want this. Holy god, but I want.

"I don't want to be alone," she whispers.

I slide my hand over her cheek, cradling her face. For a moment I just stand there, savoring the feel of her skin beneath mine, the sensation of touching someone I care about. For a moment, it doesn't matter that I'm broken, that I can't love her fully and right like she deserves.

For a moment, she is enough.

I nip her bottom lip. Her breath huffs into my mouth and I want to swallow the sensation and savor it. I press my lips to hers. She opens for my hesitant touch, her tongue brushing against mine, twining, dancing, tasting.

An erotic twist of moist, delicate strokes.

She makes a warm sound in her throat. "I live very close to here."

I am suddenly a very thankful man. "You don't mind that I've been drinking? I might not be able to get it up." The truth, hidden in an alcohol-laden confession.

"You're not a violent drunk, are you?"

I lower my forehead to hers. "Not with women."

She slides closer, her body aligned with mine. Until I can feel the inhalation of her breath.

"And we already know you're very good with your mouth," she whispers in my ear. Her breath is hot. My body shudders with arousal, dark and needy and far too long denied. I can almost imagine a shiver of sensation in the vicinity of my dick.

I smile and nip at her ear. “That was just a warm up.”

This time, it is Abby who shivers, her body trembling. I can feel the shift in her. The lithe, erotic tension twisting through her sinews, making them soft and supple.

She buries her face in my neck. “Oh god, just the thought of that is making me crazy.”

“Of what?” I whisper. “Can you say it?” I press my lips to her neck where the pulse is scattered and quick. “Tell me what you want?”

We are standing in the street, bathed in overhead light. She is pressed to me, her body as close as it can be while fully clothed.

And I have never been more aroused. More fully aware of someone else’s need, throbbing through her and into me.

It is powerful what I can do with my mouth, my words.

It is not enough.

It is everything.

Chapter Eighteen

Abby

It takes an extreme amount of confidence to whisper dark and dirty things to a lover. Even more to do it in a public space.

It requires trust to whisper those forbidden things. Those intimate, private longings we can't even admit to ourselves.

I close my eyes, holding on to the sensation of Josh's mouth on mine. The memory of his body pressed to me in the dark.

I tell my friends to be brave. To go after the brief moment of happiness they might be able to capture in the dark interludes between loving and hurting.

I tell Graham to be brave. To walk away from the violence of a lover who hurts him.

I cannot say those same words to myself. I am not brave. I cannot whisper the things I want to do with Josh. I cannot put voice to those words.

I am a coward hiding behind a carefully manufactured façade.

"Come home with me?" I whisper instead, taking the easy path to promises of pleasure.

He smiles against my mouth. "Is that the best you can do?"

"I'm not very creative."

He makes a warm sound, deep in his throat. "We're going to have to work on that."

"I think I like that plan."

I take his hand, reluctantly stepping away from him to lead him the few blocks to my apartment.

It's small but it's just me living here. I don't have a lot of furniture. I have a thing for secondhand shops, especially in this part of North Carolina where old and new money intermingle freely.

It's not Spartan, but it's functional and it's mine; the first space I've had that's totally mine. No roommate. No expectations.

Which is why there is a pile of unfolded laundry on my couch.

Josh smiles when he sees it, then draws me closer to him until there is nothing but silence and heat between us. "I knew you couldn't be perfect."

"I'm far from perfect."

"Not from where I'm standing."

"You're poetic when you've been drinking."

If I hadn't tasted the whiskey on his tongue, I wouldn't have guessed he was drunk. He isn't slurring. He isn't staggering. He's more relaxed than normal. A little more handsy in a slow, sensual kind of way.

"Can I touch you?" A harsh, guttural whisper against my lips.

"Yes please."

His lips part. His breath is a little more ragged. A little quicker.

Seeing his body tense sends a spike of need straight to where I am hot and aching for him.

"Would it be too forward if I stripped down right here?"

He smiles darkly. "Not at all. I think I would like that very much." He leans in, tracing his lips down my throat. "Especially since I can't get you to tell me your fantasies."

I press my hands to his chest, urging him backward until he sinks down to my secondhand chair in the Target slipcover.

I've never done this. I don't want to overthink it.

I turn down the lights, leaving only a faint glow from the lamp over the kitchen stove. There is enough light that we are not cast in darkness. The shadows dance over his face. I can feel the need radiating off him.

Slowly, I feed one button after another through the fabric on my blouse, peeling it open. Heat pulses between my thighs. He's watching me. It feels like a physical caress.

I turn my back on him, glancing over my shoulder at him as I slip the white fabric over my bare shoulders. First one, then the other until it falls to the floor.

He doesn't notice. His eyes are on me.

I am not afraid to do this. Not afraid to let him see me. All of me.

I unhook my pants and slide the dark fabric down

my hips, inch by inch. His gaze follows the edge of my pants as I reveal myself.

The other night, neither of us explored much. It was raw and ragged, hidden in the dark.

Not tonight. Tonight, the lights are on. Low, but on.

And they hide nothing. I can tell the instant he sees them. The raised scar on my shoulder. The starburst on my ribs that I hid with his comforter the last time.

I knew this was a risk. But tonight, I need him to see all of me. To see the perfection I can create with my smile that hides the deeper, damaged truth.

The reality of the violence that I too have lived. Not as an adult in war. No, not that.

But as a child. As a little kid made helpless by a grown man's insecurity and rage.

I am eleven years old again, trying to find the words to tell my teacher where the bruises on my arms came from.

Or to explain to the emergency room nurse how I cut my own shoulder.

But the real hurt isn't in the scars or the violence that caused them. It's in the verbal cuts that I wasn't good enough as I was. That if only I'd change who I was, I would be worthy. Loveable.

The scars are my private shame. That I wasn't strong enough to fight back. That I fell down and did not get back up. That I changed who I was, despite fighting so hard to stay the same.

I will not be that person again.

I step into the space between us and settle each of my legs on either side of his hips. My thighs are spread wide and my core, aching and wet, is separated from him by a thin piece of functional cotton that feels woefully inadequate.

He strokes his thumb over the jagged scar on my shoulder. "Looks like this hurt." The softest whisper.

"Belt buckles tend to."

He glances up sharply and there is violence in his eyes now. Restrained. The good kind of violence. The kind that lashes out to protect.

It warms the cold space inside me. And like a frozen thing seeking the heat, I cannot break away.

Josh

It is one thing to live through violence. It is one thing to be the instrument of someone else's death and to take pleasure in protecting your brothers from the evil that would do them harm.

It is quite another to see the evidence of violence etched into someone else's skin. A permanent reminder that there are things we will never outrun, will never forget.

There is nothing I can say to take away the pain she clearly lived through. I cannot make her forget it. I cannot hurt the man who hurt her.

And I'm not nearly drunk enough to do something stupid, like demand she give me his name and let me use my friends in the Army to hunt him down and make him hurt.

Instead, I do the only thing I can think to do.

I press my lips to that scar. I can feel the raised edge of it beneath my lips. The salt on her skin is sharp and tangy. Fear, laced with arousal.

People who say that scars are evidence of things you were strong enough to overcome haven't felt the weight of the shame in those scars.

I can see her wrestling with it. Struggling to keep it buried and under control.

"How old were you?"

"Eleven."

I slide my hands over her ribs. Over the starburst there and up until they are flat against her back, drawing her closer to me, until her mouth is a breath from mine.

She lowers her forehead to mine. "It was hard tonight. Going with Graham."

"You saw me get into a fight at the bar the other night. Why didn't that upset you like this?"

"I think because it wasn't…it wasn't a relationship. It…it didn't feel personal."

I am wrestling with the need to hunt this bastard down. Not just for hurting Graham. But for hurting Abby through her friend.

"Will he go back to him?"

Because that is the most likely result. At least in heterosexual relationships. No matter how committed someone is to leaving, they tend to go back. More than once. It takes years of trying to break free from a bad relationship.

I don't know if it's the same in the gay community or not.

But I know it will hurt her if he does.

"I don't know," she whispers. "He's my best friend. And I hate this."

I pull her close, tucking her head against my chest and simply holding her. The alcohol is numbing my reactions. I should be angrier. More pissed.

And I am.

At that moment, there is something more important I need to focus on.

Abby.

I slide my hands over her back. Soothing, gentle strokes. My fingertips barely skimming the softness of her back. Tracing the edge of her bra. Teasing and light, I can feel the transition my touch evokes in her.

And the stillness where my own response to her need should be.

I reach behind her, flicking open her bra and inching it over her shoulders. Her nipples are deep russet pearls against her skin. She's so fucking beautiful, she hurts my eyes.

I can't look away as I lean in, watching her reaction as I take her in my mouth. A tiny nip of my teeth against her sensitive flesh. It tightens beneath the wet slide of my tongue.

Her eyes are heavy and dark. Liquid gold. I bite down gently, cupping the soft swell of her breast as I taste her. Her lips part, and she arches a little bit in silent offering.

I trace the edge of her other nipple with my fingertip as I torment the first. Her skin glistens where I've touched her with my tongue, my teeth.

She threads her fingers into my hair, dragging her nails along my scalp. She spreads her thighs further, pressing her hot core against me. Instantly, my hand is on her, stroking her where she is swollen and moist and hot. Beneath her panties, my fingers find her. Swollen, so swollen. I drag the fabric down in a single movement.

She's so fucking wet.

I don't ask for permission. I am lost in the purity of her response. In the need to make her forget everything but my mouth, my fingers, my touch.

My name.

I slide my finger from the top of her swollen clit down the seam of her body and lower, to the tight, forbidden knot below where she is welcoming and open for me. She tenses but doesn't pull away.

Trust.

Again, I slide my finger over her body. Down. Against her tight, secret place. Until she relaxes. I flick my tongue where she is swollen and she nearly flies apart against my lips.

I suckle her, sliding one finger deep inside her wet heat. Stroke after slow stroke, I feel her relax and tighten, a sensual erotic dance.

I want her to forget her own name. Slowly, so slowly, my fingers inside her, I press my thumb against that secret, tight spot. Her eyes fly open and her cry is a thing of beauty.

But I don't stop now. Gentle, circling pressure, stroking her body with my fingers, my tongue.

But it is my thumb in that secret space that does her in. I press against her. Not seeking entry. Just a gentle, erotic slide against her most sensitive flesh.

And then she is coming apart. Beneath my finger, my lips, she shatters, her thighs gripping my shoulders. Pulling me closer and pushing me away all at once. Her breath ragged and torn from her lungs.

My heart swells in my chest as I finally relent and pull her against me. Skin to cotton. Heart to heart.

And beneath my own heart is a tiny seed of hope that maybe, just maybe, there is a chance I could get my life back. That it could be my cock inside her when she comes. That I could feel her body surround me and wrap me in the pleasure of her touch.

But for now, feeling the glow of her orgasm spreading over her like a warm sunset, I am content.

And her pleasure is enough.

Chapter Nineteen

Josh

I like her apartment. I like lying with her in the tiny space and feeling the world fall away. It's nothing like mine. It's a tiny loft with little hints of Abby scattered around it. I smile when she turns on the light and she catches me watching her.

I smile, thinking of the pile of laundry on the small couch a few feet away. "Laundry day?"

She makes a wry grin. "Had no choice. Ran out of panties."

My throat goes dry at her words. I slip my hands over her lush hips. I love her curves.

I hope she's strong enough for me and all my bullshit.

But I'm not going there. Not yet.

I lean in and press my lips to the base of her throat where her pulse is scattered. "That's a hell of a visual," I whisper.

She is pressed against me on her bed, her body wrapped in a sheet. I'm still dressed, my clothing more than a physical barrier between us.

I close my eyes. I am suddenly terrified of losing

her. But I can't do this to her any longer. I can't be selfish here, no matter how dark and lonely the night will be without her.

I've only known her a short period of time but I need her like air. I need her. Abby. She is my light in the darkness. My rock.

I hesitate, unable to speak.

Waiting. Like she expects me to tell her I've got some incurable disease and have two weeks to live.

"What's wrong?" There is fear in her golden eyes. Hesitation and warmth where there had been only warmth and desire.

I suck in a deep breath. There is nowhere for me to go. I could avoid this once more. Use my mouth to drive her to mindless pleasure.

But sooner or later, she'll figure things out. And if I'm not honest with her, if I don't tell her now, I will destroy the very woman I'm falling for.

It helps that I'm a little drunk. It makes the shame a little easier to bear.

I take her hands. I can't find the words for a long, long moment. Finally, I guide her hand to the fabric covering my useless cock.

Her breath hitches as her palm curls around me. I can feel her. A forced, cautious smile at the edge of her lips. "You don't seem very excited to see me."

I swallow the fear. God but her hand feels good on me. It's been so fucking long since anyone has touched me there. Since I've touched even myself. I close my eyes and lower my forehead to hers. "It doesn't work anymore."

She stills and says nothing. I suppose it's a victory that she doesn't pull away.

I hold my breath, waiting for her to step away from me. To leave me, alone and broken and useless.

I close my eyes, avoiding the shame. Avoiding the pain.

My lungs are tight. It hurts to breathe.

She slips her hand free from mine. My skin is cold where she touched me.

My heart shatters in my chest, breaking into a thousand tiny pieces.

I feel her move.

"I'll go."

Then she stuns me. Her palm is warm as she urges my face up. Her body is warm as she slides across me, her legs on either side of my hips. "Why on earth would I want you to do that?" she whispers.

I swallow the lump that suddenly blocks my throat. "I can't...You didn't hear me wrong, Abby. I can't..."

Her palms are warm and gentle on my skin. Suddenly all I can feel is the warmth of her skin against my cheeks.

I want to reach out. I want to touch her. But I am gutted with shame.

She leans closer, and her breath is a soft huff against my skin. She presses her lips to the center of my forehead. "I don't care."

Her words fall on disbelieving ears. She can't be telling the truth. She simply can't.

"We can't have sex, Abby." I can't look at her.

"I...you deserve someone whole. Someone who isn't a fucked-up half-man."

She presses her index finger to my mouth. "Don't talk about my friend like that," she whispers.

"That was pretty corny." I laugh weakly. "You can't tell me that sex doesn't matter to you."

"Of course it does." She shifts and rocks gently against me where I am useless and soft. "But sex is more than just insert tab a into slot b."

I groan softly at the terrible joke. "You're on a roll with bad jokes."

"Yeah, I know." She lifts my chin, her fingers pressing against my cheeks. She brushes her lips over mine, teasing and soft. "You've made me feel alive in a way I haven't in a long, long time."

I glance up at her. She is surrounded by light, her skin cast in shadows, the color of dark honey. "You're serious?"

"I guess you haven't been paying attention." She smiles wickedly. "Your penis isn't what I like about you."

I choke on a horrified laugh and drop my head to her chest. Her arms circle my shoulders and hold me. In the thousand different ways this could have gone, I never imagined it would be like this.

Because I haven't told her all of it. She only knows the part of my secret I can barely summon the courage to put into words. But she doesn't know all of my shame.

And when she finds out, there will be nothing that will keep us together. But until then, I am selfish enough that I cannot let her go.

Abby

I think I am not as surprised by his revelation as I should be. There was always something more with him, something he wasn't ready to let the world see.

In a million years, I wouldn't have guessed it would have been this.

He's young. He's healthy.

I can't imagine living with this. Not as a guy our age, when everyone else around us is talking about hooking up.

I curl into him, needing nothing more at the moment than to be where I am. I don't know what to say.

"You're surprisingly okay with this," he says after the silence stretches between us.

"You clearly overestimate the value of a penis in this equation." I lift my head to make sure he sees I'm joking.

"I have no idea what that even means."

"It means there's a hell of a lot more to sex than a penis brings to the equation." This could not be any more awkward. "You didn't just pound away like a jackhammer. So things were…well, let's just say you did everything right."

His lips quiver. "So you like what I do with my mouth?"

I swallow, thinking of him there again, his tongue against my heat. "A little bit." The words squeak out.

He draws me closer. "What about my fingers?"

Heat floods through me and I squeeze my thighs together again as the ache builds once more. "That too."

His mouth moves along my throat. "Tell me what you want?" he whispers.

I close my eyes, letting the pleasure of his touch stroke over my skin. "You have too many clothes on."

"Say, 'I want you naked, Josh'," he whispers.

It's a game. Light, teasing words to take away from the seriousness of it all.

"I want you naked." The words are almost lost in the haze of pleasure I get from his hands on my body.

"Josh."

"Josh," I repeat. My mouth is dry. "Can I touch you?"

"Yes please."

He lifts the t-shirt over his head and I watch the glory that is his body twisting and arching.

I love his chest. The way the black ink contrasts sharply with the burnt cream color of his skin.

The sheet falls from my body and I lean forward, pressing my breasts to his chest, my hand against his hard, flat stomach. His skin is warm and rough against mine. He is still as I explore the sharp edges and planes of his body.

My hand slips lower, brushing against his hip

bone. He catches me, halting my movement.

His grip on my wrist hurts.

And when I look up, it is not arousal looking back at me.

It is shame. It is sadness.

It is a thousand pieces of emotion looking back at me. "Don't."

A single word guts me. I know instantly what I've done. It hits me like a wall of disappointment.

He drops my wrist and sits up, turning away. The names on his back flex with the movement.

"Josh." He does not respond. He reaches for his pants and yanks them on. "It's okay."

He rounds on me then. "No. It's fucking not okay. It's not o-fucking-kay that I can't get a hard-on. It's not fucking okay that you still want to reach between my legs for that useless piece of skin. It's not fucking okay, Abby."

I hold the sheet to my body. It is a useless shield.

"I thought I could do this." The bitterness in his words slices at my heart. "I was wrong."

He drags the rest of his clothing on.

I am mute. Unable to take back the hurt. Unable to fix it.

Unable to find the courage to ask him to stay. To fight...for us, for this thing we were trying to start.

In that moment, I hurt him. I reminded him of everything he cannot do, even after I told him it didn't matter.

And there is no way I can make it up to him. No way to end the offense I didn't mean to cause.

And his silence makes it worse. I want him to rail at me. To tell me how fucked up it is that I assumed I could fix what doctors could not.

I slip from the bed, removing myself from the offense. Shame crawls heavy and dark across my skin as he dresses in heavy silence.

And my heart breaks into a thousand pieces when the door closes behind him. Leaving me alone.

And hurting.

Just like always.

Chapter Twenty

Josh

I had to go. I had to leave and get away from the strange disappointment in her eyes when she realized that no, I wasn't going to magically get a hard-on.

It hurt. It fucking hurt.

I knew it would. I knew we wouldn't be able to do this.

That I wouldn't be able to do this. I could fuck her six ways from Sunday with my mouth, my fingers or any of a thousand different things and it still wouldn't be enough.

And it hurts.

I default back to what I'm good at. Drinking and fighting. Except that Eli isn't at The Pint tonight. Which is strange because he's always here. It's his bar.

And now I really need to know what the hell is going on.

But Caleb is there and he's drinking hard and this is not good. Caleb drunk on a good day isn't easy to deal with.

Where the hell is Eli?

No, this is not fucking good at all.

"Funny thing about war," Caleb says as he tosses back his shot. "It's never really over."

I watch him pour another shot, feeling helpless and weak and fucking impotent. Just like always.

There's no reason to pry. It'll come out if he wants to talk. Otherwise, I'm just there to keep him from drinking alone. Because for some reason, getting hammered together is functional and okay. Getting plowed alone in a bar is something only people with problems do. At least, that's what the Army always told us in every fucking safety briefing and death-by-PowerPoint slide show on suicide awareness.

I don't miss the endless briefings. Not by a long shot.

"What do you miss about the Army?" I pour my own glass.

I have no idea why I'm sitting here with Caleb, watching as he crawls further and further into the bag.

I can't help but feel there is something different tonight. There's a darkness in Caleb that isn't usually there. Or at least I've never seen it behind the bravado and false machismo. Which is good because then I won't feel like I've betrayed everything that I ever thought I believed in by drinking with him.

"The guys. The stupid shit we used to complain about." I know what's coming. The drinking didn't work. Not as a distraction. Instead, the door is wide open for whatever is tormenting him to escape and fill the dark bar with shadows and pain. "I want it to be worth it. I want to know they died for a reason. That it wasn't some stupid boondoggle."

It hits me then that I've judged him harshly and wrongly. I never saw beyond the bullshit war stories to ask if there was anything more.

I stare into the shot glass, seeing the past and the hurt and the anger that I've tried really fucking hard to ignore the last few months since getting out. The shame that had damn near choked me after I realized I hated him because he put into words the thing I hated about myself.

"I can't say it's worth it. I wish I could." I raise my glass, a silent salute to the brothers we've lost.

It hurts. Goddamn it, it fucking hurts.

And yet, it's a familiar hurt that only someone who's been there understands. I can't drink with people from campus. They don't get it. No one does. Unless they've been there.

"You ever wonder why we went?"

I pour two more shots for both of us. "Drink. If we're drinking, bottoms up, brother."

He frowns into his glass, swirling the liquid. Some spills over the side and onto the back of his hand.

I don't know what set Caleb off tonight but now that I'm here, my own bullshit is rising up. The onslaught of anger and bitterness drowns a little beneath the haze of alcohol. I've been trying so hard.

"And yeah. It surprises me sometimes," I say after

a moment.

"Huh?"

"Like I'll be listening to the radio and a song will come on from one of my deployments and I just...I go back. This one time, we were on patrol and the LT had speakers hooked up in his truck. We're getting the shit kicked out of us and then all of a sudden Raspberry Beret comes on loud as hell. In the middle of a firefight, Prince. He never lived that shit down." I grin wickedly at the memory. People who have never been there are horrified when they realize what we can laugh at. The worst times in our lives, the blackest moments, and someone can crack a joke that will have us damn near pissing ourselves.

There's no laughter now. It's going to be a rough fucking night.

"How do you turn the shit off? When you start thinking about it?"

I don't answer for a long moment. I can't. Because my throat is blocked by something I can't swallow. And it hurts. It's like a giant lump stuck in my chest.

"I don't. Sometimes, I can distract myself by going for a run or something. Other times, not so much. That's when Uncle Jack comes into play."

He's got a death grip on that glass. "You don't like me, do you?" His voice breaks a little.

"We've all got our demons, brother."

"I know you think I'm full of shit." He smiles and it's sad and biting and cold. "I thought maybe...maybe you'd get it. More than the other guys.

You worked for the general. You know what it's like at those levels of the game."

I frown. "You were in my unit?"

A division staff is huge. And no, I don't remember ever seeing him before.

"Yeah, man. I worked for one of the brigade commanders. I saw…I know…I was there when Blackjack Nine died."

Fuck me. Blackjack Nine was Second Brigade's sergeant major. He died in a massive bombing when the insurgents started using ten-thousand-pound bombs in dump trucks.

"I'm sorry, man." What else can I say when I've been a complete prick to him?

There is nothing left to do but pour another shot. Wishing I could make the memories stop. For him. For me.

But I can't.

And sometimes, the only solution is to drink until they leave you alone.

Chapter Twenty-One

Abby

The hurt doesn't magically stop after you cry yourself to sleep. And no amount of Ben & Jerry's helps either.

I am raw and tender and bruised, and I have to somehow drag my ass to work and smile and pretend that my soul isn't lying crushed and bleeding on the ground.

I skipped classes today. Every single one of them.

But I can't skip work if I want to pay the rent this month.

And as is the way with friends, they notice when things have gone to shit, no matter how much you try to hide it.

"What happened?" Graham opens his arms and because it hurts, I go to him. He is the only thing holding me upright at the moment. "Things didn't work out with Captain California, did they?"

"How did you guess?"

"I'm psychic. A key life skill as a bartender."

I tip my head and step out of the comfort of his embrace. "Why do you call Josh anything but his name?"

I've never stopped to ask why before now. As far as I know, Graham has only talked to Josh once, that day a while ago when he was drinking before noon.

"You know that song by the Eagles, 'Hotel California'?" He sets a glass on the bar and folds the towel he'd been using.

"Yeah."

"He's in his own private Hotel California. He can never leave, no matter how much he wants to."

I lean back against the table, letting Graham's words sink in. "He'll never leave the war behind, will he?"

Graham swallows. "I don't know. I wish I did." He glances out at the darkness leading to the bar. He pauses then looks back at me. "We are the product of what we come from. But we don't have to let that dictate our choices." Graham takes a step toward me and pulls me into his arms once again. "You are the strongest woman I know."

"I'm not strong, Graham. I smile and wave and pretend to be something I'm not."

He shakes his head. "You're wrong. The whole world has been trying to change who you are. And you haven't surrendered." He pauses. "If that's not strength, I don't know what is. If anyone deserves happiness, it's you. And I don't know if Josh is the right guy or not…but I'd let him eat crackers in bed."

"Oh god, that was terrible." I burst out laughing, swiping at the tears that burn down my cheeks. "You know, for a guy who likes to pretend he's a dumb blond, you're pretty slick." I tuck my bag into the small space under the bar and tuck my shirt in. "You're also not wrong." I sigh hard, trying to release the tension in my chest. "Why does this have to be so hard?"

"Because nothing that comes easy is worth it."

"That's a shitty way of saying God has a plan or some other platitude, isn't it?"

He shrugs apologetically. "No." This time, it's Graham who pats my cheek. "I just think...that no matter what, we have to take care of each other. Even when we don't understand why it hurts."

Graham's words slither beneath my skin and strike a little too close to home.

Because for a long time, I didn't understand why people stayed in relationships that are so terribly bad for them. Part of me still doesn't.

It's easier to end things with Josh than to ever face the hurt again. To ever feel it again. "I hurt him," I whisper.

It's easier to hold on to the anger, to the hurt, than it is to figure out just what the hell had been going on that night to make him lash out like he did. I screwed up but Josh...Josh went for the jugular.

"You know how people say 'I love you' means never having to say you're sorry?" Graham says quietly. "They're full of shit. 'I love you' means admitting you're wrong. It means not just saying I'm sorry. It means trying to do better." He squeezes me and lets me go. "Do better. Take a chance. And start with I'm sorry."

This isn't going to end well. I should leave him be. Let him go. But I've screwed up badly enough that I can't let it end like this.

He'll be at The Pint. That's where he always is.

* * *

Normally, The Pint is welcoming and warm and fun, but tonight it feels like all eyes are on me, frozen in the doorway. Times like this make me feel the darkness of my skin in ways that I don't when I'm around my friends.

Josh is sitting–or rather *leaning*–at the bar.

I have never felt this before. This pain.

But it's new for me to have been the one to cause it.

Josh glances up at me, his eyes glassy. He's swaying on his feet.

I can't feel anything. All the sound stops.

All I can see is Josh.

And then he's approaching and he is all I can see. Maybe later, this will make sense.

I thought I could do this. I was wrong.

I can't. Because I'll give in to the emotions rioting inside me and I'll hurt him. That's what I do.

Josh is right in front of me now. He's more than a little drunk. His voice is thick and slow.

"I really don't want to do this right now." His voice is smooth and deep, even if his eyes are somewhat glassy from far too much to drink.

I have broken us. Destroyed the fragile thing between us that had just gotten started.

This is my fault.

Josh

She is braced for war. Braced for me to lash out, to cut her and when I do, I end her responsibility, relieve her of the pain she caused.

"I don't really want to do this right now." It is the most reasonable thing I can muster.

She needs me to forgive her. The rational part of my brain should say the words she needs and let her go.

At least now I can keep my shame buried. She'll never know she did us both a favor by ending things between us before I got too attached.

I can't think.

"I just…I just want to say I'm sorry. That's all. You don't have to accept it. You don't have to forgive me. I just need you to know."

And the words, the anger, boil out of me before I can stop them. I round on her, giving in to the anger and the hurt. Permanently cauterizing the wound. Stopping the bleeding and any chance of healing things between us. "I don't want to fucking talk about it."

God love her, she doesn't back down. "Don't you think that maybe that's part of the damn problem?"

Oh fuck this. "Do you want to talk about the choices you make with your hair? Then don't ask me to talk about the fucking war, Abby. Just don't."

If I haven't destroyed the fragile foundation of whatever it was we were building, I've done it now. I've crossed the line. Stabbed her where she is soft and vulnerable.

Hurting her so that she'll walk away.

Hurting her so she'll never have to know why I have to go.

"So you run away? The first time things get a little difficult?"

I recoil from her words. They hurt worse than if she'd lashed out and struck me. I can't stop myself from shouting at her. From lashing out. I see the hurt flicker across her face, and I am the cause. "You don't know what it's like to walk through life, to not feel any fucking thing. To feel completely cut off from everything."

I will be ashamed later. Right then, the shame and the anger and all of it comes crashing down on me. Pouring out in violence and rage at the one person in this life I care about.

She doesn't back down. She steps into my space. "Because you run away from it. You just fight and drink and hope that it'll be enough. It's not. Not if this is the way it's going to play out."

And I am over the edge of control. If this is going to end, it might as well go down in a blaze of painful honesty.

"Why can't the fact that I had some bad shit

downrange be enough?"

"Because you tell me that you're broken and the one time I screw up a little bit, you lash out at me? That's okay with you?" she says quietly. It's like she physically deflates.

It hurts. Like I'm cutting out a piece of my heart with a dull blade. "I was a goddamned fool for thinking that I could do this with you. That you wouldn't push me for more. That you could just take me for who I am."

"That's not fair." Her words are laced with hurt.

"Life's not fucking fair. It's not fucking fair that your goddamned father died. It's not fair that I made it home but my fucking dick might as well be a paperweight. Life isn't fucking fair."

She flinches but doesn't back away. I'll give her that.

And I'm going to destroy her. Because that's what I do. It's all I know. "I'm not a mind reader."

"Because I don't want to talk about it! I want to forget it. All of it. I want to come home and be fucking normal. But that'll never fucking happen." I'm gone. I can't stop. It's like the last two years have finally broken free and are tearing out of me. "You want to know why?" I back her up until she is pinned against the wall. "I was on a patrol. We got stopped. Do you know how bad burning tires smell? You can taste the burning rubber in your mouth. It penetrates your fucking skin." My fists are bunched by her head, and it is taking everything I have to not slam them into the bricks.

"You know why I have such a fucking hard time in class? Because fucking violence isn't theoretical to me. It's bleeding, pulsing, hot and raw. And here's a little something no one tells you. It feels fucking good. Really fucking good."

The memories crash over me like a wave of violent crimson blood and gore. I can hear the screams again. The cries.

The helplessness. Blood dripping between my clenched fingers as I tried to stop the bleeding. "It feels fucking good to take the enemy out. To know that your buddies are coming home and fuck those guys for bringing the fight in the first place. But we can't talk about that."

I see Abby's eyes. Wide. Filled with disgust and revulsion.

"I'm supposed to hate what I did. I'm supposed to say I only did what I did to survive. I'm supposed to hate war." I slap my palm into the brick next to her head. "Then why the fuck do I miss it? Why the fuck would I give anything to be back in the mud and the dirt and the shit?"

I see it then. The fear on her face. And I don't fucking care. I can't.

And then I feel it.

A terrifying sensation burns over my skin. It's so familiar, so long forgotten.

My cock stiffens.

A tightening, an ache. The latent edge of arousal. My dick swelling, like it's coming alive after a long winter.

From the fear I see looking back at me from a woman I'd dared to let myself love.

I yank away, a wave of nausea slamming into me.

I need to get away. I need to forget. To stop my sin even if I can't erase it.

I can never erase it. It has tainted me, corrupted the one thing that I wanted more than anything else in the world.

I will never, ever be able to forget the horrifying sensation of arousal and violence, twisting together in dark, erotic heat.

Abby

I am eleven years old again.

A grown man is screaming in my face. The demons of war etched in his skin, ripping him apart.

But eleven-year-old me did not love the man in my past.

And love is a powerful, stupid thing.

It takes every ounce of courage I have not to reach for him. To place my hand on the scarred and broken man in front of me and tell him it's not his fault.

I'm not eleven years old anymore. And I have a choice to make.

And I will not beg. I will not cry for this man.

My cheeks are wet in the shadows.

My heart broken into a thousand pieces in my

chest.

No matter how much it hurts. No matter how much it rips my soul out and grinds it into the damp pavement.

I let him go.

Chapter Twenty-Two

Josh

I should have gone home. But if I've utterly and completely destroyed everything good in my life tonight, I might as well keep drinking. And there's nowhere better to be right now than crawling into the bottom of a bottle, numbing the pain if not ending it. I have no idea where I'd even start on that one.

I knock back another shot. I've lost track but I'm pretty sure Eli is counting.

When I showed up at his apartment, he didn't judge. Didn't cuss me out for trying to take his door off the hinges at three in the morning.

He took one look at me and let me in, then poured the Jack and Coke silently.

Waiting.

He knew I'd start to spill at some point. He's creepy psychic that way sometimes. Right now, he's just drinking quietly, letting me marinate in my own misery.

I want to ask why he wasn't at The Pint tonight but I don't.

Eli says nothing. It's part of why I like the guy. The first time I met him, I pegged him for having some heavy fucking rocks in his ruck from the war. Who doesn't, though?

I sit there silently with him, filled with hate and anger and rage. Hate at the stupidity of the fucking war. Rage at the emptiness it's left me with.

And anger.

The fear that I will always be fucking damaged. That this is my new normal.

And maybe, it isn't worth it.

If I close my eyes, I see nothing but the brightly bleak desert. The piercing sunlight glinting off pools of fresh blood.

"You have any morals, Eli?" I ask finally. My words are heavy and thick and run together.

"Don't we all?"

I squint at him. He's a little blurry right now. He might have two heads. "You're the officer. Aren't you supposed to be a leader of character or some shit?"

He shakes his head slowly, sipping his Jack. "Was an officer. I'm not anymore."

"I notice you didn't answer the question. About morals?" I suddenly very much need to know the answer to my question. Even if I won't remember it in the morning.

"Sure. I've got morals."

"Where did you put them?"

"What the fuck are you talking about?"

I point my glass at him. I'm pretty sure some Jack

sloshes over the rim of the glass. "When you went to war. Where did you leave them for safekeeping?"

"You don't check your morals at the door when you sign up, brother."

Another shot slides down my throat. It's smooth now. Smooth and steadying. "Yeah, well some of us had to." I raise my glass in his direction. "Remember when you told me I should be grateful I came home?" I shake my head. "I'm not."

"You're drunk." A quiet menace in his words that I am too far gone to heed.

"Why should I be? I can't fuck without threatening to beat the shit out of someone. All I'm good for is fighting. I should enlist again. Go back to war."

I reach for the bottle. He slaps his hand over the rim of my glass. "Say that again," he says.

"I should go back to war. Let them finish what they started."

He shakes his head. "Not that part. The 'beat the shit out of someone' part."

I swallow. It fucking sucks hearing my shame put into words. "You got it pretty much covered."

"What do you mean, you can't fuck? Without violence?"

I adjust my pants. "It's…complicated."

"Try me." He slides the bottle from my hand and pours me another glass.

Shame burns my skin. My head drops back to the chair behind me.

"I thought you were seeing that girl from the Baywater," he says after a while.

I want to ask how he knows about Abby. I remember she came to the bar one night.

Shame crawls up my spine, a cold and prickling feeling. “I screwed that up tonight.”

“Is that why you’re here?”

“You could sound a little pissed at me or something, you know? This whole saintly, calm older brother thing isn’t what I need at the moment.”

He releases a quiet sigh. “I am not your company commander and I am not your father. Your daddy trauma isn’t my problem.”

“Fuck you.” But there is no threat in my words.

“At least I can.”

I flip him the middle finger. “That hurts, man.”

I say nothing. His words cut small chunks out of my remaining pride and toss them into a frying pan. I can hear them cooking, leaving me alone and ashamed.

All I can see is Abby’s face. Her golden eyes wide. Her dark skin washed out with fear.

“I got hard tonight.” The shame almost chokes me.

Eli says nothing and I am eternally grateful for his silence. Because the words are coming, whether I want them to or not.

“Abby. I was arguing with Abby. I pinned her against the wall…”

“Jesus Christ, tell me you didn’t…”

“No! Jesus no. I’d never…I left.” I lean forward, emptying the rest of the bottle into my glass and knocking it back. Needing the burn. Needing the pain to block out everything else. "I could have hurt her tonight," I finally whisper. "And I got a fucking hard-on." The words rip from my throat, tearing their way into the world.

I lower my head onto my arms. The sob breaks free, a ragged, wicked sound.

Chapter Twenty-Three

Josh

Have you heard from Caleb?

I'm not awake yet. I blink and squint again, making sure I'm actually seeing what my brain thinks is a text from Eli.

Not since last night.

Eli doesn't usually text me before noon. I sit on the edge of the bed, cradling my head in my hands. Oh god, it's going to be a bad day. My head is pounding as if my brain is trying to beat its way out of my skull with an ice pick. I'm reasonably certain a cat has pissed in my mouth.

I don't have a cat.

I need water, but my stomach is in knots, so I just sit there. Hoping my head doesn't explode. And try to remember what happened last night.

I frown, trying to remember something important from last night. It's like trying to capture a wisp of air. Thoughts slip through my mental fingers.

I wonder if I can make it to the bathroom, and please dear lord, I hope I have some eight-hundred-milligram Motrin. Civilians always laugh when I pop one of those horse pills but damn, whatever works, right? At that moment, I'd probably cut off my little toe if it would make the pain in my head stop.

My vision is blurry as I stumble to the bathroom, and holy hell, past me is a fucking saint. A bright white pill and a glass of water are waiting for me on the counter near the bathroom sink. My stomach isn't happy with the pill, but I couldn't really give a shit at the moment. I need to get my ass to campus.

I sit up and rub my hand over my face, then read the text again.

The phone rings. "What's wrong?"

Eli isn't known for irrational panic, so the fact that he's on the other end of the phone actually does trigger worry in the hung over pit of my gut.

"Have you seen Caleb since last night?"

I frown at my phone. "I just sent you a text. No, I haven't." I think.

"Go check on him."

Eli doesn't ask much of me. Hell, I think the only thing he ever usually asks of me is that I don't break any furniture when I get into fights.

He's never asked why I fight so much and for that, I love the man.

Shame crawls over my skin as I mentally divert my brain away from that painful subject and hop in the shower. Ten minutes later, and I'm on the road to Caleb's place.

The first thing that hits me is the smell. I fucking hate the smell of piss. My stomach is already twisted from being hung over and the wall of piss smell crashes over me the second I step through the front door.

I gag then push through it. I've been in worse, much worse, and this is Caleb. And this is my penance for being a prick.

I find him on the floor of his bathroom. His pants are around his ankles, like he fell off the toilet. His entire body is spasming, shivering violently.

I rock his shoulder, trying to jolt him awake. His skin is blazing hot and dry.

"Caleb. Come on, man."

It isn't the first time. It probably won't be the last.

Because I recognize all too well how bad those nights can get when you try to handle them on your own.

Unless I start feeling more normal around civilians, I'm going to stick with people who speak my language. And the way things are going, that isn't going to happen any time soon.

"Ah hell, man, come on, get up." I try to lift his shoulders. He's shivering violently.

I might be combat lifesaver-qualified but my skills don't include alcohol poisoning.

I have no idea what to do other than keep him from choking on his own vomit.

It's an ugly thing to see your friend staring into the abyss and knowing there isn't shit-all you can do for him except sit with him.

And hope that this too shall pass.

He blinks but he's not seeing me. I have no idea

where he is but he's not with me.

I call 911. They're pretty quick in getting the details.

I get his pants pulled up and cover him with a blanket. I have no idea if he's going into shock or what.

But I sit with him.

And start talking, hoping that maybe some part of his brain can hear me.

"So hey, this is pretty shitty, you know that, right?" I've got him leaning against me. He's shivering and mumbling incoherently. "I mean, if you were trying to make me feel bad for being a dick, you could have just told me."

He makes a noise. Like he's actually heard me.

"I hope you feel bad. I'm missing class for this."

He shudders violently. I don't know what the hell I'm supposed to say right now. I mean, please don't die? What if it has the opposite effect of are we there yet? I don't want to put him on a fucking speed pass to heaven. Or hell. Hell might be where we're all headed.

We don't have a lot of stories about where soldiers of bullshit wars go when they die.

We know where the heroes go. But we're not heroes.

"Where do you suppose we go when we die?" I ask him. "I mean, we're not exactly modern-day heroes. We didn't fight the good fight. We weren't fighting the Nazis or liberating France." He's shivering again. Fuck. "I mean, the guys in the

Greatest Generation get a speed pass straight to Saint Peter, right? But what about us? I mean, we don't have a noble cause." I grip him tighter. Clearly I'm making both of us feel a hell of a lot worse.

Counselor material, I am not. Where's Eli when I need him?

He makes another noise and this sounds vaguely like an attempt at speech.

I hug him tighter as a violent convulsion steals his ability to function. "Ah fuck, man. Stay with me."

Sirens and flashing lights announce the arrival of the paramedics.

I tell them what I know. Show them the bottles of alcohol he consumed.

I stand on his front step and watch them drive away.

Another payment to the butcher's bill.

Chapter Twenty-Four

Josh

They won't let either of us back because we're not family. And no amount of lying will convince the nurse to tell us how he's doing. Eli has called in a favor with a friend who knows a guy on the hospital board.

And so now, we wait.

The waiting room at the university hospital is a depressing place. There's a young mom trying to get her toddler to stop screaming. His back is arched and his face is bunched up, his little lungs pushing all of his rage and fury out into the world.

"I know how he feels."

I glance over at Eli's quiet remark. "Caleb had two empty fifths at his apartment."

"I know. I was trying to convince him to go to a group session at the hospital."

I'm used to feeling this useless.

Eli is not.

The big man is hunched over, his shoulders bent, his fists knotted together and pressed to his mouth.

"If you knew he had a problem, why did you

serve him?"

"Because at least if he's drinking at my bar, I can keep an eye on him," he says. "What a fucking disaster."

I lean back in my chair.

And we wait.

The hours tick by.

"Does he have any family?" Eli asks after a while.

"Not that I have contact info for."

The war at home isn't fought only by soldiers. Guess this is part of it. The process of coming home.

"I thought we were supposed to win if we made it home." The words hurt. They don't even try to conceal the pain, the lies we were told. All the pictures of the happy couples, all the smiles, all the support, the troops signs and posters and military discounts.

They're a lie. A fucking lie. All of it.

"We did win."

His response is not what I'm expecting.

I can't help thinking of my limp dick, the useless fucking skin between my legs. And how fucked up that the only way it appears to want to work is if I jerk off to a war film.

What the fuck is wrong with me?

"How do you figure?"

He hesitates a long moment. "We're alive. We came home. And I fucking promise you that every Gold Star family would give anything to have their loved one back."

I sniff, trying to swallow the bitterness that

threatens to choke me. "So why doesn't it feel like a victory?"

He grips my shoulder. "Because we're sitting in an emergency room, hoping one of our buddies doesn't die from alcohol poisoning. There's no commander to hand this off to, no work to try and forget about it at." He pauses, his eyes dark, his mouth pressed into a hard flat line beneath the scruff on his jaw. "But I wouldn't trade it, any of it, even if it meant I wasn't sitting here right now."

"You have no regrets? Nothing you'd change?" My shame, the dark and twisted helplessness, is back.

Eli is as calm and steady as he's always been since I've known him. "There are different choices I wish I'd made but I can't change them."

I haven't had that certainty of purpose since before I actually encountered my first firefight. Everything since then has been vague, well inside the moral grey area that exists in war.

The nurse comes out and takes the poor mom and her screaming toddler to the back. The immediate sense of relief from the people around us is palpable.

"Hope they get him taken care of," I mumble. I can't imagine what she's going through right now. My own heart relaxes a little bit when he's no longer screaming in the waiting room, but it's not from annoyance.

No, I've heard screams like that before.

And holy fuck, I am not going down that path of

memory lane. Not tonight, not ever again.

"They've got a really solid pediatric unit here," Eli says.

"You're pretty tied into the local community, huh?" I need a distraction. Something, anything to keep the memories that started circling around that little boy's screams.

He shrugs. "No more so than any other local businessman."

"They don't do write-ups on other local bar owners in the New York Times." It was how I found his bar. There was an article about an Iraq war vet who opened his bar in the old tobacco district and had created a space for student veterans to find each other.

It worked. It's how I met him and the rest of the guys. Unfortunately, it's how I met Caleb, too, but hey, no one's perfect.

"Just doing my part, you know?"

"Yeah." I cover my mouth with my hands. "You know what I regret the most about the war?"

"What's that?"

"That it's over." I can feel the silence settle over him like a blanket. He says nothing for a long moment. "Things were simple. Life. Death. Eat. Sleep. Nothing any more complicated than that."

And it was the simple things that are laden with the most regret. At least in my life they are.

"We came home, brother. We can't go back. We–you, me–we've got people here counting on us." He jerks his chin toward the door separating us from whatever they're doing to save Caleb's ass back there.

I want to argue with him. To tell him that maybe his tour downrange was some Hollywood tour where no one had to make a bad call.

"I've been thinking…about your problem," Eli says after a few minutes.

"Oh lovely." I lean my head back on the chair and close my eyes. "I'm not really in the right frame of mind for this conversation."

"Tough shit. We're here tonight because Caleb couldn't have that conversation so you're going to fucking listen to me." I open my eyes to see him scrubbing his hands over his face. "You know fantasies aren't reality, right?"

"Oh god can we please not do this right now?" I swallow. "Isn't this a fun topic?"

"I'm fucking serious."

"I know that." I sigh heavily. "I know they're not reality."

"Then why the fuck did you freak out?"

"It's not exactly a time for rational action when you start to get a hard-on in the middle of a fight with your girlfriend." I sit up and adopt a terrible British accent. "Hmm, let me pause for a moment and consider my response. I don't really want to hurt her, therefore, the blood rushing to my penis must be caused by something else not tied to a sadistic fantasy."

He grins. "That's not funny."

"Tell me about it. You're not the one getting a

murder boner around your girlfriend."

He glances over at me. "Look, all I'm saying is that maybe you should talk to a doc about this."

I make a rude noise. "Sure. And everything will magically be solved with some antidepressants. That or they'll take all my information and lock me away in a psych ward so I don't become the next Hannibal Lecter."

"This is quite possibly the most fucked-up conversation I've ever had."

I grin because he's right. It is fucked up. But then again, everything is. I'm in the waiting room at the hospital for a guy I don't particularly like; I'm getting fucking hard-ons thinking about hurting a woman I care about. "The only way this whole night gets more fucked up is if you tell me you committed war crimes or something," I mumble.

Eli goes silent and still. Only a moment and then it's gone beneath a flash of a quick grin. "Nah. My trauma is much more mundane."

But I can't deny what I just saw.

And suddenly, my inappropriate hard-on feels a lot more insignificant.

But a doc comes out who agrees to talk to us.

And it's time once more to set aside my own problems and focus on someone else.

Abby

I'm standing in the emergency waiting room. I wish Graham hadn't told me where I could find Josh. I should probably ask him how he knew in the first place. But that can wait.

I wish I was smart enough to leave him alone.

But…I know how this ends. And when your friend is in the hospital, you go. No matter how mad or how much it hurts.

"You okay?" Graham asks.

"Not really." I let the hate flow through me. Hate for the war. Hate for the Army. Hate for the systems that fail our soldiers year after year after they come home from war.

The coming home videos are a lie. A carefully manufactured moment for everyone to feel good about. No one sees the drinking. The long nights alone. The anger. The distance.

I wish they were true. Oh god, how I wish Josh could get his happily ever after.

And as much as he ripped my heart out, he's the only one who made me feel beautiful and loved for who I was, not who he wished I could be.

My heart hurts.

"You ready for this?" Graham whispers. I love him for being moral support.

"I don't think we ever are." I straighten and wipe my hands on my pants.

"You know this is all your fault," he says with a grin. "Why couldn't you find one of those well-adjusted Greek billionaires who are into S&M?"

I choke on a horrified laugh. "I'm not really sure how to respond to that."

He laughs. "Just trying to help."

I suck in a deep breath again. "You know how they say God doesn't give you more than you can handle?" I glance over at him. "I wish he didn't trust me so much."

"You and me both, sister."

"Stay with me?" I swallow a hard lump in my throat. "In case I break."

"You won't break. But I'll stay."

We walk down the halls toward Caleb's room. I'm glad they let us back without much trouble. And by not much trouble, I mean they search my purse, but not Graham's pockets. I'm too tired and worn down to even summon the anger over the disparity. Maybe someday. But not right now. It's not worth the fight.

I pause at the edge of the curtain separating Caleb's space from the other bed. Eli meets us and pulls Graham into a quick man hug. "Thanks for coming down," he says to Graham.

I frown. "I didn't realize you knew each other."

"Eli is trying to poach me away from the Baywater," Graham says. "I'm about ninety percent on board." He pauses. "Is Josh still here?"

Eli nods. "He's going to be pissed at me for this. But sometimes…sometimes." He clears his throat and glances over my shoulder.

Josh is stopped at the end of the corridor. A

shadow in the brilliant fluorescent light.

For a moment, I think he is going to walk away. That he is going to turn and leave me standing there before I get any chance to say anything at all.

I don't want to do this with an audience, though.

Graham squeezes my shoulder as I slip away.

A thousand emotions flash over his face as I walk toward him. A million more crash through me.

Was it only yesterday I'd seen him? Only yesterday that he'd resurrected all my fears, all the nightmares from my past.

I can barely breathe. But I will not run away. I will not be weak and cowering.

I stop in front of him. "I wanted to check on you." My voice is thick and rough with fear.

"I..." For a moment I think he's going to tell me to leave. That he doesn't want me here.

I try to take a deep breath and brace for the fresh renewal of hurt.

I don't know what he'll say. What can he say that will take away the hurt?

"Can we go somewhere?"

I nod. Because I cannot walk away from this. However it ends, I need to know there is nothing I could have done to save things.

I step into the cool darkness. The air is heavy and moist. I want a sweater and a cup of coffee.

I want to keep walking. But I don't. Because I need to know. I need to know why.

I stop near a bench. Close to the bus stop. Near the stairs to the parking garage where those who can't afford a valet walk to their vehicles.

My heart is tight in my chest.

I'm waiting. For the hurt to get worse.

For the end of what we might have been.

My heart hurts from the loss, but I've got too much pride to beg him to tell me what happened between us.

Part of me, the part of me that is always waiting for the people in my life to let me down, has adopted an I told you so mentality. That this was bound to happen, and it's better that it happened now before I really fell hard for him.

But the other part of me hurts and the hurt is real and painful and worse than anything that ever happened since I lost my dad.

That maybe, this time would be different.

I was wrong. I always was.

I sit next to him on the small bench. Close enough that I can feel the heat from his body. Close enough that I want to curl into him.

Now, though, he's sitting beneath a street lamp. His head is down, cupped in both his hands as rain mists down around him.

I'm afraid. I wish I wasn't, but I've seen this movie. The one where the naïve fool approaches the guy she's worried about only to discover he's some soul-stealing vampire or something.

But I'm not that girl anymore, and I will not be afraid of monsters in the dark.

There isn't a monster looking back at me. There is only despair.

My heart cracks a little, even though I'm pissed at him.

Only now, there's an edge of fear mixed in it. Because I cannot think of anything else to do, I sit next to him. I pick up his hand and thread my fingers with his. It's such a simple, empty gesture.

"Are you okay?"

"I don't know." Josh makes an ugly sound. His fingers tense around mine. Silence stretches between us. His hand is heavy on mine. Heavy and rough and solid. Warm and real. He's here. And that's got to mean something, right?

Silence again. Until I cannot hold back the question burning inside me.

He drags his hands over his face, leaving them there. It is forever before he speaks.

It's a long moment before he shifts and leans forward, resting his arms on his knees. Finally he glances over at me. "I found him at his place." His throat moves as he swallows. "Two empty fifths."

"I'm sorry," I whisper. Because I am. Despite my anger at Josh, he is hurting right now. And Josh…I'd already started thinking of Josh as mine. And I hate it when people hurt those I care about. "I guess we have to be grateful that you were there for him," I say finally. Because I cannot ask him the question burning inside me.

"I don't want to do this anymore, Abby," he whispers finally. He glances up at me. "I want to get on with my life. To forget about the war. About the friends I lost. I want to be a normal college guy trying to hook up with girls who are too good for me. I want to drink too much for no fucking reason at all, not because I'm trying to keep the thoughts from coming. I want to worry about grades and tuition and whether the girl I'm crushing on likes me back."

It is infinitely stupid to allow myself to feel his pain, to care about his hurt. I wrap my arms around his waist and lean against him. He rests his cheek on the top of my head. I wish there was something I could tell him that would magically make it all go away. That would lift the burden from his shoulders and let him be all those things he wanted to be. But then he wouldn't be Josh.

But maybe if I figured out how to lighten his load, maybe we could lighten mine a little, too.

"Maybe that's not how life works for people like us," I say when I'm sure I can speak without embarrassing either of us by crying.

"Why not?" he whispers. "Why can't we just forget all the bad shit and live for the now?"

"I don't know." My fingers slip beneath his shirt to press against his back. "But I wouldn't change who you are." His shoulder is warm and solid beneath my cheek.

"I would gladly trade who I am to be a normal well-adjusted guy with a working cock." He lowers his forehead to mine. "I'm so goddamned sorry, Abby."

I say nothing.

He simply sits, his body, his life, threaded with mine as the rain starts to fall around us.

Chapter Twenty-Five

Josh

Fear is a powerful thing. And when you've been up close and personal to violence, it is not an abstract thing.

My stomach knots at the idea of hurting her.

Of getting hard from her pain…My skin crawls.

She shivers against a chill.

I'm stymied. I want to pull her close, to keep her warm and safe.

I want to see if I can feel anything with her, other than the arousing allure of her pain.

I do the only thing I can.

It is enough. She breaks a little, sagging against me. I am at once broken and whole.

I rest my head against her soft curls. I'm home. I'm safe.

And for the moment, so is she.

Holding her is the closest thing to peace I've found since I've been home. I cannot let her go.

But I owe her the truth. About me. About what happened.

"I panicked." God but those words are hard. My

throat closes off. I can barely breathe.

Her arms tighten around me. "I don't understand."

I can't say the words. I can't admit what the fight did to me.

"Walk with me?" Because maybe the words will be easier if I'm in motion.

When she leans back, though, her golden eyes are shining bright with unshed tears.

I cup her cheek, brushing my thumb over her smooth dark skin. "Don't cry. Please don't cry."

I pull her close again.

"I'm so tired for crying over people I care about."

"Don't cry for me," I whisper. "I'm not worth your tears."

She leans back and swipes at her cheeks. "Don't talk about my friend that way."

"That was pretty corny." I manage to smile and it feels so foreign, so unfamiliar; it feels like it could shatter my face.

She shrugs. "It's the best I can do on short notice."

I kiss her because I can do nothing less. I mean it as a teasing kiss, something easy and light, to heal the wounded space between us.

But it morphs into something else.

Something that touches the dead space inside me and makes me want to try once more to step out of the darkness and into the light.

I capture her sigh, breathing her in, needing every gasp of air she breathes.

It is torture to break away but I have to do this.

Now before I lose my last shred of courage.

Brushing my thumb across her cheek, I ease back. Tucking her fingers into mine.

"You already know about my, ah, problem." God but this is hard.

We walk, down the sidewalk cast in shadows. My skin is cold and tight.

I slip my hand from hers.

"It…yesterday." I clear my throat. "Turns out I've got an S&M streak." A bad joke. Black humor to mask the pain.

Shame burns hot beneath the cold.

"Josh." A whisper.

I clench my fists at my sides. "I…I don't know what I've become." My lungs burn. "My temper. I wanted to lash out yesterday." I can't say it. The words are stuck. Lodged in my throat. "I got hard. For the first time in more than a year, I got fucking hard."

She doesn't move. Doesn't react. The words are not a relief. They hurt, tearing free from my throat like broken glass.

"When you were afraid…" I can't breathe. The world is closing in, pushing me back into the darkness and the dead space where I've been living. This is worse. So much worse than the helplessness I've felt before. "I got off on your fear, Abby."

I can feel the shadow of the war. I can feel the relentless pleasure at the violence, the joy that we were still alive. I cannot move, cannot fill my lungs.

The war finally broke me.

And turned me into a monster.

Abby

I've seen this before. The fear, the tension. He is gone away, some place I cannot follow.

I cannot leave him alone.

Everything falls into place now. Everything makes sense. His revulsion. His reluctance.

His flight after I screwed everything up by thinking there was some magical cure.

I hear the words, let them sink in and wrap around me. I can't explain it. But the pain on his face, the shame carved into the lines around his mouth. "This is not who you are," I whisper.

"It's defined everything I've done since I got home." Words laced with pain. He does not want to take pleasure in pain.

"It doesn't have to."

And for that, I love him a little more.

But that does not mean I am safe.

I want to put my arms around him. Hold him close while the nightmares come.

But I can't.

I have seen this nightmare before.

I have lived it.

But I am no longer eleven years old.

I will do better.

"Josh."

I don't touch him. I can't reach him right now.

And I have no way of knowing if he would feel my hands on him or if he would think they belonged to his nightmares.

"Josh." I breathe out quietly. "Look at me." A whisper. A prayer. An urgent hope that he can hear me.

That he will open his eyes and see me.

It is forever and a moment more before he opens his eyes. They are dark, darker than the shadows that are normally hiding there. His mouth is pressed into a flat line.

"I'm sorry," he whispers. "I'm so fucking sorry."

I step to him then. The man beneath my hands is as hard as forged steel. Slowly, I slide my fingers over his cheeks until they slip around his neck. His hair is softer than any man's should be.

He does not resist as I draw him closer, down until there is no space between us. No air, no light. No room even for the regrets that mark us both.

It is a long moment before his arms slide around my waist. His fingers press into the small of my back and for a moment I feel utterly safe and protected.

It is forever before either of us moves. If we live to be one hundred, I won't know. But there is a moment when everything shifts. When my arms around him cease being about comfort and morph into something more. Something dark and alive and pulsing with life.

Heat floods me. I nuzzle the soft skin at the edge

of his ear. His arms tighten around me and one of his hands drifts lower to squeeze my ass. I am aching and raw. This. This is need. This is want.

He inhales sharply, then releases a quiet huff of breath on my neck a moment before his teeth scrape across the sensitive skin of my throat. I make a sound. It might be pleasure. It might be pain or a little bit of both. I arch against him–my hips to his, my neck exposed for his taking.

I don't care that we are in public. I don't care that his hands are kneading and tight on my ass.

All I care about is the tension in this man. The arousal pulsing through his body and into mine.

"I want you naked," I whisper. Because I cannot be passive. Not even now.

Whatever it takes.

"You pick now to talk dirty to me?"

I laugh and then I can no longer think. His body rocks slowly against mine. He cups my cheek and kisses me hard then, his tongue sliding against mine in a dark, sensuous caress. Telling me more in that moment than any words could ever hope to convey.

I am lost in him. The fierceness of his kiss. The ragged need in every scrape of his teeth and stroke of his tongue.

It is Josh who steps back. Who creates distance between us, a silence filled with rough breathing and the violent pounding of my heart.

"We'll get arrested," he whispers against my mouth.

"I can think of no one I'd rather have prison sex

with."

A laugh tears out of him. "We have got to work on your dirty talk."

I cup his face and pull him close.

Because after everything, I can't believe we are still standing.

Chapter Twenty-Six

Josh

Eli asks me to sit with Caleb for a while. For once, I am okay with it. I can't explain it. The dead space inside me feels a little less empty.

The shame…the shame is not gone. I don't think it ever will go away completely.

But there is something else crowding it out. Something pushing it away from the center of the space it occupies.

Forgiveness. Tonight, in Abby's arms, I found a moment's peace.

It won't last. It never does. Healing what ails me will take a lot more than getting hot and bothered in public.

But hey, at least I got a little hot. That's always a plus.

Caleb is fiddling with the tape holding the IV to his arm. He looks a hell of a lot better now that he's no longer dying. It always does something to the complexion, that whole not-dying thing.

Finally he glances up at me. "So you and Abby, huh?"

It's a desperate attempt at a normal conversation when we've never really had one before. I don't even think to ask him how he knows her name.

"Yeah."

"She's cute," he says quietly. I brace, waiting for him to comment about the color of her skin. Instead he says nothing.

"Yeah, she is." I swallow the unexpected lump in my throat at the reminder of how I met her.

"So what happened?" I finally ask.

"I don't honestly fucking know." His words are sharp and biting. Not the defensiveness of a junkie hiding his latest fix. The anger of someone who screwed up and doesn't know how. "After we went out, I couldn't sleep. I kept drinking. And the next thing I know, I wake up here."

My stomach twists. The memory is too fresh, too real, too close to a fucking disaster for me to pretend it doesn't matter. I rub my hands over my mouth. "Jesus."

"Yeah. I fucked up." He rubs his hand over his face. His eyes are bleary and bloodshot.

"I need a fucking drink," I mumble.

"That makes you an alcoholic."

"I'm only marginally less fucked up than you are." I flip him off.

"I knew I liked you."

I laugh and it silences the voice in my head for a moment. I notice him flexing his arm. I don't think he even realizes he's doing it.

There's more to Caleb's story; that's for damn

sure. Then again, there's always more to our stories. At least, that's what I've always figured. The guys who won't talk about it are the ones who dealt with some shit.

I tip my head toward Caleb. "I thought you were tied into the VA since you came home?"

He shakes his head. "They keep canceling my appointments." But he looks down the street, away from where I'm standing.

I don't push. Maybe I should. But I can't get past the noise in my head. And there's no room in my rucksack to carry any of the rocks from his.

I've got my own wounds that are scabbing over.

I grip his shoulder silently. There's really nothing I can say. Nothing appropriate, anyway.

"You should talk to the doc."

"I did. They gave me more meds." I can't take the pain away. But he can forget for a little while.

"Sounds about right." He's waiting for a more extreme reaction from me. He's not going to get one. I'm all for whatever it takes to get by out here.

"I can't function." He's braced. Waiting for judgment and condemnation. "I've been trying since I got home. I fucking can't do it."

"So what's the problem? You're going to one of the top schools in the country and you're doing fine. I fail to see the problem here if you need a little help sleeping or managing the anxiety."

Caleb doesn't answer. Not for a long moment. I'm not sure what rabbit hole he's gone down. All I can do is wait for him to come back up. No matter what.

Because that's what we do. We stick. We don't fucking run out on people who matter to us. No matter how broken, how fucked up. We stand together. Shoulder to shoulder.

I think that's the part I miss the most about being in. It's what I've been looking for since I got here.

Caleb finally looks up at me. "I guess it's not okay if I have to spend the rest of my life liquored up just to go get out of bed every day." He pauses, rubbing his hand over his mouth.

I look down at my hands. I can't help but wonder what I wouldn't trade to have a drinking problem and working dick.

But I can't tell him that.

Finally I glance up at him. "I can't tell you what the right thing to do is." I press my lips together, hoping I've got the right words. "But whatever you decide, me and Eli and the guys…we'll be here."

He nods. And yeah, I get it. People don't know what it's like to have a family like the one you get in the Army. The people who will drop everything and fly halfway around the world if you need them.

Or who will sit in a hospital with you as you try to figure out if you're going to take the red pill or the blue pill.

Abby

The rain is falling outside, sparkling sheets of

grey in the street lamps. I'm sitting with Graham in the waiting room…just waiting for whatever comes next.

"What are you thinking?"

I look up at Graham's cautious question.

"I don't know."

"After all of this, Josh better be worth it." He pauses. "Or else I'll have to kill him."

"I think he is." I swallow and look over at him. "But it hurts. And I don't think love is supposed to hurt like this." I lean against him, resting my cheek against his shoulder.

"How the hell did I end up like this, Graham? I wanted a nice, normal, well-adjusted guy and instead I end up with a former soldier. There's nothing I can do to fix things. There's nothing I can do to make it stop. I'm just stuck on a treadmill to nowhere with the men in my life."

"He went to war, honey." He squeezes my hand. I can't believe Graham is defending him but there you go. "He's allowed to be a little messed up."

"I love him," I whisper. "I want to keep loving him." I cover my mouth with my hand. "But what if that's not enough?"

He hugs me close. He can't protect me from this and he can't make my decisions for me. "I don't know."

I should be happy that Josh and I are talking. And I am. I really am.

But I am terrified that I know how this story ends.

Josh steps into the waiting room. He looks ragged and tired. There are dark bruises beneath his eyes. Shadows there, looking back at me. Graham squeezes my shoulder. "Go. I'll see you at work tomorrow."

I am rooted to the floor as Graham steps out of the waiting room.

It's far too easy to cross the small space to where Josh is standing. To slide my arms around his waist. To feel his arms tighten around my shoulders, and breathe in the warm smell of his skin.

"Come home with me?" A simple, loaded question. One that I may regret. One that I can't resist.

"I'm afraid." His voice is a quiet rumble beneath my cheek.

"I know."

I tip my chin up and draw his mouth down to mine. I don't care that we are in a public place. I need to feel his mouth on mine, to remember what it's like to feel his touch, his taste. I need to feel alive and Josh is the only one who can do that for me.

His tongue slides against mine as his fingers curl around my neck. My belly tightens. I press against him, needing, wanting. He lowers his forehead to mine. "I'm sorry. So goddamned sorry."

I breathe deeply, trying to keep my heart from breaking in my chest. "Me too."

We stand there a moment, until a nurse asks us to move. He twists his fingers in mine and we step out of the light and into the darkness.

But we are together.

And that makes all the difference in the world.

Chapter Twenty-Seven

Josh

I shouldn't have come home with her. I should walk away and leave her and never look back.

I stand there in the entrance to her apartment. I will only hurt her. It's what I do.

But I cannot walk away. Not tonight.

Because I am afraid to be alone.

I can't breathe. I can't see.

"Josh."

I stop. It hurts. Christ this hurts.

She wraps her arms around my waist and simply holds me. She is strong and solid and real, more real than the pain squeezing my heart and threatening to cut off air to my lungs.

I want to turn and wrap my arms around her but I am frozen. She is all I can feel, the center of my world. Her hands rest over my heart and for a moment, I am whole again.

When I can move, I rest my cheek against her hair, reveling in the soft, cool curls against my skin. She smells warm and sweet and like the brief moment of sunlight in the darkness of my world. I need this. I need her and I cannot muster the words I need to tell her that. To beg her not to turn away from me.

Not to leave me alone.

Not tonight. Not when the demons are circling, reminding me of everything that I've done and failed to do in this life.

If there is a hell, I'm living in it.

Because now I can remember what it felt like to get hard. To feel aroused by the beautiful woman in front of me.

And now there is nothing again. No signs of life between my legs.

She reaches for me, penetrating the loneliness that blankets my skin like a shield. Her fingers slide beneath my shirt. They're warm, stroking over my skin.

Promising something that can never be.

I grab her wrists. Gently, so gently. "There's nothing there, Abby."

She twists her wrists free, her fingers tracing over my abdomen. I shiver beneath her touch. She arches into me, rubbing her hips against mine in a forgotten rhythm. "I want to feel you," she whispers against my lips. "Skin to skin." She brushes her lips over my mouth, nipping my bottom lip. "Lie with me?"

Fear is a powerful thing. But the idea of curling around her, pulling her body flush against mine, the softness of her skin against mine…it's a powerful temptation.

And it's harmless.

I cup her face in my hands and kiss her then, pouring everything I cannot say into that kiss. Slowly, she pulls me toward her bedroom. It is her space and I am filling it, taking it over.

She is consuming me. Her fingers slide my t-shirt over my head. I stand there, exposed and vulnerable. I can't remember the last time I removed all of my clothing in front of a woman. My gut clenches tight as her fingers flip open the button of my jeans. She nibbles on my bottom lip as she drags her nails across my hips, pushing my pants down with the back of her hands.

I close my eyes as the air kisses my cock. She presses her lips to my hip bone. I fight the urge to thread my fingers through her soft, curly hair. God, but the idea of her on her knees in front of me drives me a little bit insane.

Instead, I fist my hands by my sides. Letting her take the lead. Letting her do what she likes.

I step from my pants. I am naked. And she steps away from me. Light filters in through the blinds. Light slices over her skin, an erotic dance as she slowly, so slowly, slides her hands up her own hips. Over her ribs where she catches the hem of her blouse and slides it up, slowly, over her skin.

Inch by glorious inch, she exposes herself. Her skin is bathed in soft shadows and light, a dark, dusky softness I want to taste.

I move to her. Drop to my knees. Her skin is soft and warm beneath my touch. I press my lips to her belly. Lick her a little, all while watching her. Her golden eyes darken a little. Her lips part. I love watching her. Doing this to her.

It doesn't matter that nothing works for me. It only matters that she feels. That she arches beneath my mouth, my tongue. Her fingers slide over my scalp.

I rest my head against her belly for a moment. Just a moment. I savor the feel of her pulse beneath my cheek. I drag her slacks down over her hips and legs and then she is as naked as I am.

"You're so beautiful." I draw her down against me.

She is soft where I am hard, smooth where I'm rough. I feel the heavy weight of her breasts against my chest, her belly against mine. Her neck is warm beneath my lips, her pulse hammering against my lips. "Lie down," I whisper.

She tries to draw me down with her. I shake my head. "On your belly."

She arches one eyebrow. I kiss her softly. "Trust me."

She swallows, then turns slowly, so slowly, away from me. Watching me as she crawls onto the bed, her body exposed and open for me.

She lowers her shoulders, leaving her hips arched high. For a moment I can imagine standing behind her, sliding into her where she is warm and tight. I can almost feel her body pulsing around my cock as I slip deeper inside her.

It is a fantasy I would kill to fulfill.

Instead, I run my hands over the smooth curve of

her ass, then urge her down, lower, until her hips are pressed into the bed.

I want to hold her. To savor her.

But that will never be enough.

I lean forward and press my lips to the small of her back at the center of her spine.

And shatter a little more.

Abby

I shiver the moment his lips touch my spine. I can't help it. There is something illicit about his hands caressing my hips and his mouth just there in the small of my back.

His breath is warm against my skin, a stark contrast to the comforter that suddenly feels too rough. I don't usually notice the air, but tonight, I can feel every stir of it against my flesh.

His legs have trapped me. Rough and hard, they're pressed to the outside of my thighs. I press mine against his, trying to spread them, a silent offering.

He makes a noise, deep in his throat. His palm is hard on the curve of my ass, sliding down over my skin, achingly close to the place I want him to touch me. To fill me.

He urges my thighs apart, just a little. The cool air kisses me where I'm wet and hot. His hands slide over my inner thighs, closer, closer. I arch a little more, begging silently. He brushes a single fingertip over the seam of my body. I can feel the slickness there and I want him, any part of him, inside me.

I make a sound, a whisper. A plea. I don't know any more. I can't say. I am lost in sensation as he teases me. His lips, his fingers. He's driving me closer to the edge. Closer to coming, all without touching me where I need him to touch me.

"Please." I'm not above begging now.

But he simply makes that noise again, his palm sliding closer then further away. Close again, a single finger teasing me, just along the edge. My thighs are wet now, my entire body alive with sensation. Pleasure.

My fingers twist in the comforter.

And all the while, he simply slides his fingers closer, away. His lips trace small bites over my shoulders, the blades of my back, while his fingers tease me. He nuzzles my hair out of the way.

And then he moves. All at once. He bites down on the edge of my neck where I am soft and sensitive while he fills me. Two fingers slide inside my body–finally, finally.

I shatter. I come apart at the edges, rocking against his fingers as he moves them inside me, touching me where I need him so desperately. The orgasm rockets through me again and again, twisting me apart, dragging me under until I forget everything–all the hurt, all the pain, everything but Josh. Josh's lips. Josh's fingers. His big body surrounding me until I am lost.

Drifting and silent, my body hums. His fingers are inside me, moving slowly, guiding me slowly, slowly back to earth. To my bedroom.

To him.

When I am no longer vibrating, when my body no longer shudders as his fingers fill me, he slips them gently from my body. I try not to notice the emptiness now.

And then he pulls me against him, his chest to my back, his thighs cradling mine, his arms surrounding me.

I squeeze my eyes shut tight, unwilling to spoil the moment with tears.

Unable to stop the hurt that I know this will bring.

I thread my fingers with his and draw his hand between my breasts.

Never have I felt so loved, so cherished.

This. This is why I stay. This is why I can't leave.

This.

Chapter Twenty-Eight

Josh

I hate waking up and not knowing where I am.

My heart slams against my ribs. My hands shake as I breathe deeply, trying to control the panic that rips through me.

I suck in a deep breath and inhale a warm, familiar, comforting scent.

Abby.

I move my cheek a little and she is there. Curled into me, her body soft and warm in sleep.

I turn into her, needing the comfort of her body, her scent, to drive away the latent edge of panic. Slowly, so slowly, the panic fades, leaving in its place something else.

Something aching and warm.

At first, I don't believe it. I can't.

I feel like I am twelve years old again as I reach down between our bodies, needing my hand to confirm what my brain is telling me.

That it's not a fucking dream that will turn into a nightmare when I wake up and see my dick soft and useless once again.

I'm awake. I'm really awake.

And I've got a fucking hard-on.

There is something like joy inside me. Like there should be doves released into the sky and holy organ music filling the air.

It's hard not to sit there and just hold it. To feel it hard and smooth in my hand. I should feel awkward at best, stroking my cock with Abby right there.

I want to wake her up and be all "look at my fabulous erection".

But that just feels weird. And a little sad. Because nobody is ever as excited about your own erection as you are.

And I'm afraid if I stop, if I do anything other than lie there, stroking myself slowly, that it'll go away, fading back to being nothing more than a memory.

I squeeze a little tighter. My balls clench at the sensation. Christ it's good, so fucking good to stroke my cock again. I make a noise, deep in my throat. Something like pleasure, long forgotten.

And then I feel Abby move. She shifts in the bed, rolling toward me. I pause.

I don't know if I should be guilty or proud or ashamed. Heat flashes over my body.

And she nuzzles my neck, her hand sliding down my belly over the sensitive head of my cock to grip me gently.

I almost come right then and there. My balls tighten. I'm there. So close. I want this to last, to not end. To never end.

But her hand is sliding up and down my cock, tugging in just the right place, tightening now, twisting, until I unload, coming on my belly like I might tear apart into a thousand tiny pieces.

"Christ." A prayer. A profanity. I don't know. I can't think. I can only feel as she keeps stroking me until I'm sure I'll die from pleasure.

"See," she whispers, when I'm no longer certain I'll embarrass myself by crying. "You don't have an S&M streak after all." She nuzzles my neck again before nipping my earlobe.

I can feel it already. A stirring, a tightening.

I pull her against me, needing the contact. I am suddenly more afraid now. More terrified that this might be a fluke.

Or that now, I will disappoint her.

She kisses me then, her hand sliding over my cock, caressing the head of it, wet from my own cum.

"Abby."

"Shh."

She slips her thighs over mine. "We need…"

"I don't have any." I want to cry. "I haven't needed them in so long, I just stopped carrying them around." I close my eyes, not wanting to admit that I'd given up hope of ever being where I am at this exact moment.

She lowers her forehead to mine. "I might cry."

She laughs, tucks her face against my neck and laughs.

But then she shifts and slides her warm, wet heat along the length of my cock.

My entire body burns with the need to be inside her. To feel her surround me.

I grip her hips gently.

And ease her away. "We can't. Not without protection."

She smiles at me. "You really are a saint, aren't you?"

"Not really." I draw her lips to mine. "I just don't want anything to risk what you've worked so hard for."

She blinks rapidly then and kisses me fiercely.

She presses her lips to my throat, my collarbone. I go absolutely still as she inches her way down my chest.

I can't breathe. I can't move.

I can't look away.

She is there, her mouth just there. Her breath is warm on my cock.

And then her mouth, moist and warm and soft, surrounds the tip of my cock, sucking it gently, so gently.

I can die a happy man. She tightens her fist around the base–squeezing, stroking, sucking me.

I can't resist. I thread my fingers through her soft, curly hair and try so fucking hard not to move. Not to hurt her.

But the sensation surrounds me, drags me away from all conscious thought, until all I can feel, until everything I am is focused on that single sensation of Abby's mouth on my cock.

And then I'm lost, gone, coming again, harder

than I've ever come before.

Lost in the unbelievable feeling of finally being home.

Abby

I don't want to go to class." I want to get our happy asses to the drugstore and get some condoms and spend the rest of the day in bed.

Josh is laughing at me. "I'm the one who should be saying that, not you."

I want to throw something at him for laughing. "Listen, Mr. Magic Fingers. You've been teasing me for days now. And I'm supposed to be all 'let's go to class and talk about symbolic violence' when you've finally decided to get an erection?"

I crawl into his lap, pushing him away from where he was tying his shoes. He grips my hips and drags me closer to him. "I'm not laughing at you," he whispers against my mouth.

And then he kisses me. Hard. Harder than he's ever kissed me. My lips are bruised. If they're not, they should be.

I want more. I want it all. The pain. The pleasure. With Josh there are no half measures.

"You really want to be a responsible adult?" I whisper.

"No. I think we need to at least pretend to be responsible adults." He smiles against my mouth.

"And the clinic is on the way to class. So we can take care of our little problem on the way back here."

"I'm surprised you're being so rational about this."

"I'm really not. It's more self-preservation than anything. If I don't go to class, I might get calluses from jerking off too much today."

The laugh breaks free, and I lower my forehead to his. It feels so foreign to laugh like this with a lover. To laugh with Josh.

I cup his cheek, his stubble soft beneath my palm, and kiss him sweetly. I want to cherish this. Because the darkness isn't gone. It's merely waiting, lurking. I know it will be back.

It always comes back.

But for the moment, I will ignore it. I rock against him gently. "Class ought to be interesting today."

"Why?"

"Because I've never been distracted by the possibility of sex afterward."

"Probability," he growls against my mouth. "This is going to happen."

"Only if you can get it up."

A sound wrenches out of him. Something between a laugh and a snarl. He rolls then until I am pinned beneath him. Until I feel the weight of him between my thighs, the hard length of him rubbing against my core where I am already aching for him again.

"I'll get it up," he says. Then he closes his eyes and rests his forehead against mine in what is becoming an achingly familiar gesture. "I hope."

"You will. And if not? We've always got your fingers."

He laughs again and we finish dressing for class.

It's going to be a long day.

Chapter Twenty-Nine

Abby

It's strange to no longer feel alone as we sit in Quinn's class. I'm no longer surrounded by a sea of people who act like they are never quite sure if they should approach me or pretend I'm not there.

It's fine. I'm used to it.

But I'm not used to this. To having him next to me. To feeling his strength and warmth beside me, knowing that later, as soon as class is over, we can leave.

We can finish what we started.

I'm aching and distracted as Quinn starts his lecture. Parker is there, asking her normal rational choice theory-based questions. She's not even annoying me today.

I guess this is what it feels like to have a lover that consumes everything. All your thoughts. All your fears. Everything.

Josh is taking notes. He's slouched back in his chair, his notebook leaned up at an angle. I'm not sure if he's actually taking notes or if he's doodling.

I love the way his fingers wrap around the pencil.

The thick tip guiding the pencil across the page.

I can all but feel that finger on my skin, sliding over the seam of my body.

He glances up at me. Heat flushes across my skin as he catches me staring. His lips quirk in a tiny smile, just a crease at the edge of his lips.

Yeah, I'm not paying attention at all.

"What can we say about religious versus secular violence?" Quinn asks, drawing my attention away from the promise of Josh's hands.

His fingers stop the movement of the pencil.

Just like that I can feel the shift in Josh.

But the class keeps going on, as though the world hadn't just frozen beside me. Parker raises her hand. "I'm not sure I see a difference."

Josh is tense beside me.

I cautiously raise my hand. "I think we need to break it down into smaller categories than religious versus secular violence."

"What would you propose?" Quinn asks me.

"I'm not sure. I think we'd need to dissect violence conducted by the state, violence conducted by individuals acting on behalf of another institution." I take a deep breath. "And violence conducted by individuals on their own behalf." My words fade a little. I hate myself for it.

Josh glances over at me, a question in his eyes. I shake my head a little bit, focusing on the lecture, refusing to go backward ever again.

He leans over; his breath is hot on my ear. His words rumble over my skin. "Save whatever frustration you have for later."

I duck my head and smile. Nice distraction. I write on the edge of my paper.

"Is there a difference in those levels of violence? In the forms they take?" Quinn pauses. "Mr. Douglas?"

Josh shrugs. "I don't know. Does it matter why someone kills? If the end state is the same?"

There is an undercurrent in that question, a darkness I'm afraid to acknowledge.

But I've already seen it. I've already looked at this man and seen what he's capable of.

"Our legal system acknowledges a difference in intent," Parker says.

There's something off in her tone today. There is something in her voice that lacks her normal spark, and damn it, I do not want to care.

"How so?"

"We don't punish people strictly for killing. We punish people for intentionally killing," she says.

"Durkheim famously said crimes are the things we punish because we punish them, not because they are inherently criminal in and of themselves," Josh says. And I try not to be impressed that Josh knows anything about Emile Durkheim, my favorite sociologist. "So maybe it's only intentional killing we punish because maybe that's the only form of killing we wish to condemn."

Parker shakes her head once more. "Then why don't we punish soldiers? They are intentionally killing."

"On behalf of the state," I clarify.

"People who join the military do it for some sick thrill," Parker says. "We know there are higher rates of psychopathy in the military population. Why do we have to explain their killing with justifications for state violence?"

Josh is practically vibrating next to me. "And corporate board rooms have the highest rates of psychopathy and CEOs destroy far more lives than any gun-welding soldier ever will."

"That's not true," Parker snaps.

"It is. Just because the truth makes you uncomfortable doesn't make it a lie," he says.

I can feel it again, the urge to diffuse this tension building in Josh. "We've surrendered the right to take people's lives to the state in modern democracies."

Josh shakes his head. "No we haven't. It's just a convenient lie we tell ourselves." His voice is tense, but calm. Not even close to that first day where the violence practically radiated from him. "Any one of us in this room could kill someone."

"That's definitely not true," Parker says.

"It's absolutely true. How else can you explain how entire nations are moved to commit genocide," Josh says. "It's an indictment on being human, not individual character flaws."

Parker opens her mouth, then snaps it closed. It really is a banner day if Josh has finally won an argument with her.

"Any one of us could be gunned down on our

walk home from class today. We could be shot by a robber or hit by a drunk driver. We tell ourselves our lives are safe but that's because we live in a bubble. A nice protected world where the police don't shoot us for the color of our skin, where the streets are safe to walk at night. Or where religion is something done on Sundays or Fridays or whenever but not something worth dying for." He pauses. "This entire conversation is informed by very western, educated ideas. The rest of the world doesn't work like this."

"Does anyone wish to challenge Mr. Douglas's assertion that ours is a very western conversation?" He looks to Parker, who is strangely silent.

Josh

I can't think straight. I keep hearing Parker's voice mocking me, my brothers. The pain that Caleb is going through right now–all dismissed as the needs of a group of psychopathic killers.

I look down at my hands. The anxiety is back. Paralyzing me, choking off my ability to breathe.

I hate this class. I fucking hate it. It is a mantra in my head, repeating over and over ad nauseam. I hate how this class makes me feel. Nothing has changed.

I doubt it ever will.

Class can't end soon enough.

Abby deserves an explanation, but I have to get

away. Have to break free before I completely lose my shit. Again.

One fucking comment. One goddamned discussion in class and I'm a fucking basket case all over again. I might as well join Caleb in the funny farm.

I feel rather than hear Abby fall into step next to me.

I am not a small man but she keeps up easily.

She doesn't stop me. Doesn't try to get me to confess my sins or talk to her or beg me to tell her what's wrong.

No, not my Abby.

She just walks with me, keeping pace as I try to outrun the demons that have followed me home from war.

I cut through a narrow, wooded path. Toward the old tunnel that leads through the dry riverbed toward my apartment.

Finally I stop. In the center of the trees, with the smell of damp woods and old leaves surrounding me, I stop.

Because I can't go on. Not like this.

"You should know I've fired my weapon in combat," I say quietly when the words will finally come.

"If you're asking me not to judge you, I already don't."

"I don't need you to." I bow my head. "I judge myself. I sit in these classes and I remember how sure I was. How satisfying it was to pull the trigger and see the bodies drop." I can't breathe. "I celebrated. I high-fived my buddies every single fucking time we made it back from a mission without getting blown up." God but those feelings–those things I had been so certain about at war–I was no longer certain about them any longer. "I walked away. When it hit me how fucked up it was that we were celebrating, I left the Army." I hand my head, unable to hold it up. "Part of me misses it. Fiercely."

I doubted. And I hate the fucking doubt. I hate how it makes me feel dirty.

Like a monster, cloaked in the flag and worshiped for his service.

I feel her move a moment before the warmth of her hands penetrates the ice around my heart.

I can't stop. I have to tell her. She has to know. Someone has to know.

And if she walks away, then so be it. But I can't do this with her, knowing the weight of the lies I carry with me. That haunt me.

"I never regretted any of them. I never thought about their families. I never thought about whether they had a dog or a brother or a sister." I can't look at her. Can't bear to see the shame. The judgment. "I didn't care. It wasn't my job to care. It was my job to kill them before they killed me."

I finally, finally open my eyes. I see the shadows in her, the resigned press of her lips into a flat line. "I sit in class, and it resurrects everything, Abby." I suck in a deep, heavy breath and it does nothing to break the knot around my heart. "And it hurts. It fucking hurts. There's no fucking parade. There's no celebration. Just doubt. Did I do the wrong thing?

Did I make a good kill?"

Her eyes are filled now but she doesn't pull away. "I keep waiting for you to walk away. For you to say you know what, this fucked up GI with the broken dick isn't worth the effort." I shake my head slowly, fighting desperately to keep the last of it contained. Because it might just break me. "But you're here. And I can't figure out why." I grip her wrists and lower them from my chest. "You should go. Leave and go find some normal well-adjusted college guy. Preferably with a working cock and a clean conscience."

She makes a horrible sound, somewhere between a laugh and a sob as she buries her face in my neck. "I hate that you're hurting," she whispers. "I hate that I can't fix this for you." Her breath is warm on my neck. "But please don't tell me to leave. Don't push me away before we even have a chance to try." Her lips are soft against my skin. "And you do just fine, cock or no cock. We can always buy you a strap-on if it's that big of a deal."

It's my turn to make the horrified sound. I pull her tight against me, clinging to her. She is solid and steady and real. I grind my thumb and forefinger into my eyes. "That is quite possibly the most fucked-up thing you could have said." But I'm laughing, despite the pain, despite the hurt and the doubt.

She leans back, her hands light on my sides. "I think we have a date, don't we?" Her hand slides down the front of my pants. "Something about taking your cock for a test drive."

"I might die if you don't stop with the bad jokes." But her hand feels good, driving away the darkness, leaving only the soft pleasure of her touch.

"But they made you smile," she whispers.

I kiss her then, my tongue sliding deep, filling her, tasting her, telling her without words what I can never say.

Because she did more than make me smile. She brought me back into the light.

Chapter Thirty

Abby

What about these?" Josh holds up a box of red-hot-flavored condoms. Who knew the prophylactic aisle at the drug store had gotten so risqué?

I lift one eyebrow and try not to laugh. "Those are not going anywhere near my girl parts."

He slips his index finger into the waistband on my pants and tugs me forward. "What, you don't like the idea of a fire pussy?"

"No, no I don't. I imagine it's somewhat like Icy Hot and that just doesn't strike me as a good idea." I have never in my life done anything like this. It is awkward and funny and sweet.

I brush my lips against his mouth. What is meant as something light and teasing turns suddenly serious. Heat snakes down my belly and I very much want to be out of here. "Can we just get some and go?"

It's bad enough that the clinic had been closed today for inventories or something.

"I think that's a good idea." His voice is thick and rough, all teasing gone.

We get what we need and leave. It is a painfully long walk to my apartment.

Then I close the door behind us. I turn the lock. And then we're standing, together, apart. Not quite touching, not quite not. His chest is there, brushing against mine. I am afraid to move. Afraid to break the spell.

Afraid to face what I feel for this man. It is twisted in the heat and the promise of pleasure.

"I don't really know what comes next," he whispers against my mouth. He is still barely touching me, his hands hanging by his sides.

"Tab a into slot b?"

He grins and just like that the spell is broken. He threads his fingers into my hair, pulling me against his mouth. Tasting, his tongue a slow glide against mine. I lean into him until I fall against him. His arms come around me, pulling me close. The space between us disappears and I resent my clothing and his.

"Are you ready for this?" I whisper. I need the answer. I need to know this is the right thing–for him, for me.

"I've never been more ready in my entire life." He cups my face. "I need you, Abby. Only you."

"I—that's nice to hear," I whisper. Because it is. I don't know how to hear it, how to really feel those words but they vibrate across the space between us and settle around my heart.

He kisses me then and I'm not sure I said the right or the wrong thing as he lifts me and carries me the short distance to my bed.

"How about you tell me what you want?" he whispers. His long body is pressed to mine. The urgency is still there. Still potent and simmering just beneath the surface.

I slip my fingers beneath his shirt. His skin is hot and smooth beneath my touch. The hair on his belly is springy against my palm as I slide my hand lower, lower. Under the band of his pants.

I have never seen such pleasure on a man's face from a simple touch. His eyes are closed, his lips parted. His breath is rough and ragged as my fingers close around him. He's not quite hard, not quite soft. I squeeze him gently and beneath my touch, he swells, stiffening.

"I want to touch you." The words are strange, filled with urgency and need.

He flicks the button open on his pants, giving me access to his cock. He thickens as I stroke him. His hands fall away, clenching at his sides, letting me set the pace.

"I love it when you touch me," he whispers. "It feels so fucking good."

"I love touching you." I lean in, my lips near his ear. "It gets me wet."

He jerks as the words drift over his skin, his hips rocking gently in time with the slip of my hand over the moist tip of his cock.

I release him and push his t-shirt over his head. Then his pants are gone and he's there, naked and glorious in front of me.

"Tell me, Abby." His breath is hot against my skin.

It doesn't last. The moment my pants hit the floor, he is behind me, his big body surrounding me.

It doesn't last. I can feel him, hard and urgent against my ass. I rock my hips against him. He shivers. "Do that again."

I slowly, so slowly, slide my hips against his. His cock is nestled between my cheeks, pressing somewhere intimate and unfamiliar and erotic.

"Christ, you're driving me crazy."

He turns me in his arms, lifting me until his cock is pressed to my core.

"You have no idea."

It is torture watching him roll the condom into place, wondering how this will go.

And then he steps back between my thighs. "I want to watch," he whispers against my mouth. "I want to watch my cock slide into you. I want to watch you come."

I twist my arms around his neck and kiss him, hard, drawing him close until his cock presses against my heat, sliding against my clit where I am aching and swollen. I need this. I need him. I rock my hips, and he slides against me again, the sensation erotic and new.

He scrapes his tongue across my throat, nipping gently. He nips at my breasts and pleasure spikes through me, hot and needy. "Please."

He drops to his knees, and I close my eyes at the sight of him between my thighs. "Beautiful," he whispers.

Then he touches me with his tongue and I am lost.

Josh

She is beautiful when she comes. Her lips part and the shivers run through her body and into my mouth. She tastes like vanilla and honey. I could feast on her for days, just to watch her come again.

I love that I get to share this with her. That I am the one tasting her, teaching her how it feels to have a man's mouth on her pussy. It's something I never considered before but with Abby, everything is about discovery. For her and me.

I slide one finger into her where she is tight and wet and pulsing. I want her ready for me. The idea of hurting her, even during sex, is enough to make me shrivel. But I stroke her, with my tongue, with my fingers, driving her closer to the edge a second time.

She's making tiny noises in her throat, mewling, urgent sounds that are driving me a little crazy. I reach down, stroking my cock, the condom sliding over my skin. My balls tighten and I'm close, too damn close.

I kiss her belly, her deep, dusky rose-colored nipples, her throat, finally claiming her mouth as I edge my cock where she is calling for me.

She wraps her arms around my back, her thighs

tight around my hips. "I want you inside me."

I cup her neck, lowering my forehead to hers as I slide a little inside her. She's tight, so fucking tight. "Oh god."

A prayer. A curse. A plea. I have no idea. The pleasure overwhelms me. It's been so fucking long since I've felt anything remotely close to this.

She is heaven. Tight and squeezing and pulsing. I slip my thumb over her clit, stroking her as I slide into her fully, deeply.

Her breath is unsteady and quick. Her breasts rise and fall with her quick gasps.

"I can die happy now," I whisper.

"Don't you dare." Her words against my lips. Her legs slide around my hips and she rocks against me, urging me to move. Slipping from her body, then back in, slowly, slowly feeling her adjust to me. Claiming me fully.

"More."

Her head drops back, her nails dig into my shoulders. I'm driving into her now, losing myself in the rhythm, the tiny cries she makes as the distance between us is consumed until there is nothing between us but sound and sex and belonging.

This. This is where I belong. With Abby.

My balls tighten and my orgasm rips through me. I am lost. I am found.

I am home.

"I love you." The words tear from me. I am clinging to her. To the life she has brought me back to.

She releases her nails from my back, slipping her

palms over my skin as she pulls me close.

Her response slides over my ear and wraps around me, a balm on my heart.

“I love you.” The words I didn’t know I needed to hear.

Epilogue

Abby

I understand now. I understand what it means to find someone who fits you and what it means to love them no matter what.

I understand what it feels like when someone loves you for who you are. Not who they want you to be.

I know Josh isn't done dealing with everything from the war. I know there will be more dark times.

But as I step into the darkness and find him waiting for me after my shift, I'm willing to take the chance. I'm willing to walk through the darkness with this man.

I press my lips to his, my heart full tonight.

"What's that for?" he asks.

"Just because."

His lips crease at the corners just like they did when I first met him. "Sounds like a pretty good reason," he says lightly. He cups my cheek and deepens the kiss and I don't care who is watching. "Hungry?"

"Starving." I brush my thumb over his bottom

lip. "I don't have to work tomorrow."

"I'm supposed to say let's be responsible adults and study for our exams." He brushes his nose against mine. "But instead, I'm going to suggest we stay in bed all day."

I make a tsking sound. "I'm not sure how I feel about you leading me down the path of irresponsible behavior."

"I know how I feel about it." He leans close until his breath is hot on my ear. "I can't wait to hear you make those sounds you make when I'm inside you."

Heat slides over my skin and settles between my thighs. "We won't talk about the expression you make when you're getting ready to..."

He claps his hand over my mouth. "I'm not secure enough in my manhood for you to start picking at my masculinity."

Beneath his hand, I laugh, then slide my arm around his waist as we walk down the dark path away from work.

I don't know where things are going with him.

I only know that I love him enough to go with him. Into the darkness.

And hope there will be enough light to guide our paths.

More Books by Jessica Scott

Thank you so much to everyone who has ever bought one of my books, emailed me or just stopped by the blog, twitter or Facebook just to say hi.

Reviews help other readers decide whether or not to pick up a book. If you'd consider leaving one, I appreciate any and all reviews.

Want to know when my next book is available or special sales? Sign up for my newsletter at www.jessicascott.net

If you'd like to read more about soldiers coming home from war, please check out my HOMEFRONT series: Come Home to Me, Homefront, After the War & Forged in Fire.

If you'd like to read about my own experiences in Iraq and the transition home, please check out To Iraq & Back: On War & Writing and The Long Way Home: One Mom's Journey Home From War.

Keep reading for a special look at Before I Fall, book one in the Falling Series

Before I Fall

Chapter One

Beth

My dad has good days and bad. The good days are awesome. When he's awake and he's pretending to cook and I'm pretending to eat it. It's a joke between us that he burns water. But that's okay.

On the good days, I humor him. Because for those brief interludes, I have my dad back.

The not so good days, like today, are more common. Days when he can't get out of bed without my help.

I bring him his medication. I know exactly how much he takes and how often.

And I know exactly when he runs out.

I've gotten better at keeping up with his appointments so he doesn't, but the faceless bastards at the VA cancel more than they keep. But what can we do? He can't get private insurance with his health, and because someone decided that his back injury wasn't entirely service-related, he doesn't have a high enough disability rating to qualify for automatic care. So we wait for them to fit him in and when we can't, we go to the emergency room and the bills pile up. Because despite him not being able to move on the bad days, his back pain treatments are elective.

So I juggle phone calls to the docs and try to keep us above water.

Bastards.

I leave his phone by his bed and make sure it's plugged in to charge before I head to school. He's got water and the pills he'll need when he finally comes out of the fog. Our tiny house is only a mile from campus. Not in the best part of town but not the worst either. I've got an hour before class, which means I need to hustle. Thankfully, it's not terribly hot today so I won't arrive on campus a sweating, soggy mess. That always makes a good impression, especially at a wealthy southern school like this one.

I make it to campus with twenty minutes to spare and check my e-mail on the campus WiFi. I can't check it at the house – Internet is a luxury we can't afford. If I'm lucky, my neighbor's signal sometimes bleeds over into our house. Most of the time, though, I'm not that lucky. Which is fine. Except for days like this where there's a note from my professor asking me to come by her office before class.

Professor Blake is terrifying to those who don't know her. She's so damn smart it's scary, and she doesn't let any of us get away with not speaking up in class. Sit up straight. Speak loudly. She's harder on the girls, too. Some of the underclassmen complain that she's being unfair. I don't complain, though. I know she's doing it for a reason.

"You got my note just in time," she says. Her

tortoise-shell glasses reflect the fluorescent light, and I can't see her eyes.

"Yes, ma'am." She's told me not to call her ma'am, but it slips out anyway. I can't help it. Thankfully, she doesn't push the issue.

"I have a job for you."

"Sure." A job means extra money on the side. Money that I can use to get my dad his medications. Or, you know, buy food. Little things. It's hard as hell to do stats when your stomach is rumbling. "What does it entail?"

"Tutoring. Business statistics."

"I hear a but in there."

"He's a former soldier."

Once, when my mom first left us, I couldn't wake my dad up. My blood pounded so loud in my ears that I could hardly hear. That's how I feel now. My mouth is open, but no sound crosses my lips. Professor Blake knows how I feel about the war, about soldiers. I can't deal with all the hoah chest-beating bullshit. Not with my dad and everything the war has done to him.

"Before you say no, hear me out. Noah has some very well-placed friends that want him very much to succeed here. He's got a ticket into the business school graduate program, but only if he gets through Stats."

I'm having a hard time breathing. I can't do this. Just thinking about what the war has done to my dad makes it difficult to breathe. But the idea of extra money, just a little, is a strong motivator when you don't have it. Principles are for people who can afford them.

I take a deep, cleansing breath. "So why me?"

"Because you've got the best head for stats I've seen in a long time, and I've seen you explain things to the underclassmen in ways that make sense to them. You can translate."

"There's no one else?" I hate that I need this job.

Professor Blake removes her glasses with a quiet sigh. "Our school is very pro-military, Beth. And I would consider it a personal favor if you'd help him."

She's right. That's the only reason I was able to get in. This is one of the Southern Ivies. A top school in the southeast that I have no business being at except for my dad, who knew the dean of the law school from his time in the army. I hate the war and everything it's done to my family. But I wouldn't be where I am today if my dad hadn't gone to war and sacrificed everything to make sure I had a future outside of our crappy little place outside of Fort Benning. There are things worse than death and my dad lives with them every day because he had done what he had to do to provide for me.

I will not let him down.

"Okay. When do I start?"

She hands me a slip of paper. It's yellow and has her letterhead at the top in neat, formal block letters. "Here's his information. Make contact and see what his schedule is." She places her glasses back on and just like that, I'm dismissed.

Professor Blake is not a warm woman, but I wouldn't have made it through my first semester at this school without her mentorship. If not for her and my friend Abby, I would have left from the sheer overwhelming force of being surrounded by money and wealth and all the intangibles that came along with it. I did not belong here, but because of Professor Blake, I hadn't quit.

So if I need to tutor some blockhead soldier to repay her kindness, then so be it. Graduating from this program is my one chance to take care of my dad and I will not fail.

Noah

I hate being on campus. I feel old. Which isn't entirely logical because I'm only a few years older than most of the kids plugged in and tuned out around me. Part of me envies them. The casual nonchalance as they stroll from class to class, listening to music without a care in the world.

It feels surreal. Like a dream that I'm going to wake up from any minute now and find that I'm still in Iraq with LT and the guys. A few months ago, I was patrolling a shithole town in the middle of Iraq where we had no official boots on the ground and now I'm here. I feel like I've been ripped out of my normal.

Hell, I don't even know what to wear to class.

This is not a problem I've had for the last few years.

I erred on the side of caution – khakis and a button-down polo. I hope I don't look like a fucking douchebag. LT would be proud of me. I think. But he's not here to tell me what to do, and I'm so far out of my fucking league it's not even funny.

I almost grin at the thought. LT is still looking after me. His parents are both academics, and it is because of him that I am even here. I told him there was no fucking way I was going to make it into the business school because math was basically a foreign language to me. He said tough shit and had helped me apply.

My phone vibrates in my pocket, distracting me from the fact that my happy ass is lost on campus. Kind of hard to navigate when the terrain is buildings and mopeds as opposed to burned-out city streets and destroyed mosques.

Stats tutor contact info: Beth Lamont. E-mail her, don't text.

Apparently, LT was serious about making sure I didn't fail. Class hasn't even started yet, and here I am with my very own tutor. I'm paying for it out of pocket. There were limits to how much pride I could swallow.

Half the students around me looked like they'd turn sixteen shades of purple if I said the wrong thing. Like, look out, here's the crazy-ass veteran, one bad day away from shooting the place up. The other half probably expects the former soldier to speak in broken English and be barely literate because we're too poor and dumb to go to college. Douchebags. It's bad enough that I wanted to put on my ruck and get the hell out of this place.

I stop myself. I need to get working on that whole cussing thing, too. Can't be swearing like I'm back with the guys or calling my classmates names. Not if I wanted to fit in and not be the angry veteran stereotype.

I'm not sure about this. Not any of it. I never figured I was the college type – at least not this kind of college.

I tap out an e-mail to the tutor and ask when she's available to meet. The response comes back quickly. A surprise, really. I can't tell you how many e-mails I sent trying to get my schedule fixed and nothing. Silence. Hell, the idea of actually responding to someone seems foreign. I had to physically go to the registrar's office to get a simple question answered about a form. No one would answer a damn e-mail, and you could forget about a phone call. Sometimes, I think they'd be more comfortable with carrier pigeons. Or not having to interact at all. I can't imagine what my old platoon would do to this place.

Noon at The Grind.

Which is about as useful information as giving me directions in Arabic because I have no idea a) what The Grind is or b) where it might be.

I respond to her e-mail and tell her that, saving her contact information in my phone. If she's going to be my tutor, who knows when I'll need to get a hold of her in a complete panic.

Library coffee shop. Central campus.

Okay then. This ought to be interesting.

I head to my first class. Business Statistics. Great. Guess I'll get my head wrapped around it before I meet the tutor. That should be fun.

I'm pretty sure that fun and statistics don't belong in the same sentence but whatever. It's a required course, so I guess that's where I'm going to be.

My hands start sweating the minute I step into the classroom. Hello, school anxiety. Fuck. I forgot how much I hate school. I snag a seat at the back of the room, the wall behind me so I can see the doors and windows. I hate the idea of someone coming in behind me. Call it PTSD or whatever, but I hate not being able to see who's coming or going.

I reach into my backpack and pull out a small pill bottle. My anxiety is tripping at a double-time, and I'm going to have a goddamned heart attack at this rate.

I hate the pills more than I hate being in a classroom again, but there's not much I can do about it. Not if I want to do this right.

And LT would pretty much haunt me if I fuck this up.

I choke down the bitter pill and pull out my notebook as the rest of the class filters in.

I flip to the back of the notebook and start taking notes. Observations. Old habit from Iraq. Keeps me sane, I guess.

The females have some kind of religious objection to pants. Yoga pants might as well be full-on burqas. I've seen actual tights being worn as outer garments and no one bats an eye. It feels strange seeing so much flesh after being in Iraq where the only flesh you saw was burned and bloody…

Well, wasn't *that* a happy fucking thought.

Jesus. I scrub my hands over my face. Need to put that shit aside, a.s.a.p.

Professor Blake comes in, and I immediately turn my attention to the front of the classroom. She looks stern today, but that's a front. She's got to look mean in front of these young kids. She's nothing like she was when we talked about enrollment before I started. She was one of the few people who did respond to e-mails at this place.

"Good morning. I'm Professor Blake, and this is my TA Beth Lamont. If you have problems or issues, go to her. She speaks for me and has my full faith and confidence. If you want to pass this class, pay attention because she knows this information inside and out."

Beth Lamont. *Hello, tutor.*

I lose the rest of whatever Professor Blake has to say. Because Beth Lamont is like some kind of stats goddess. Add in that she's drop-dead smoking hot, but it's her eyes that grab hold of me. Piercing green, so bright that you can see them from across the room. She looks at me, and I can feel my entire body standing at the position of attention. It's been a long time since a woman made me stand up and take notice. And I'm supposed to focus on stats around her? I'll be lucky to remember how to write my name in crayons around her.

I am completely fucked.

Chapter Two

Beth

It doesn't take me long to figure out who Noah Warren is. He's a little bit older than the rest of the fresh-faced underclassmen I've gotten used to. I'm not even twenty-one, but I feel ancient these days. I was up late last night, worrying about my dad.

I can feel him watching me as I hand out the syllabus and the first lecture notes. My hackles are up – he's staring and being rude. I don't tolerate this from the jocks but right then, I'm stuck because Professor Blake has asked me to tutor him. I can't exactly cuss him out in front of the class.

Which is really frustrating because the rest of the class is focused on Professor Blake, but not our soldier. Oh no, he's such a stereotype it's not even funny. Staring. Not even trying to be slick about it like the football player in the front of the classroom who's trying to catch a glimpse of my tits when I lean down to pass out the papers.

Instead, our soldier just leans back, nonchalant like he owns the place. Like the whole world should bend over and kiss his ass because he's defending our freedom. Well, I know all about that, and the price is too goddamned high.

And wow, how is that for bitterness and angst on a Monday morning? I need to get my shit together. I haven't even spoken to him and I'm already tarring and feathering him. Not going to be very productive for our tutoring relationship if I hate him before we even get started.

I take a deep breath and hand him the syllabus and the first lecture worksheet.

I imagine he's figured out that I'm his tutor.

I turn back and head to my desk in the front as Professor Blake drops her bombshell on the class.

"There will be no computer use in this class. You may use laptops during lab when Beth is instructing because there will be practical applications. But during lecture, you will not use computers. If your phones go off, you can expect to be docked participation points, and those are a significant portion of your grade."

There is the requisite crying and wailing and gnashing of the teeth. I remember the first time I heard of Professor Blake's no computer rule. I thought it was draconian and complete bullshit. But then I realized she was right – I learned better by writing things down. Especially the stats stuff.

I look up at Noah. He's watching the class now. He's scowling. He looks like he might frown a lot. He looks…harder than the rest of the class. There are angles to his cheeks and shadows beneath his eyes. His dark hair is shorter than most and he damn sure doesn't have that crazy-ass swoop thing that so many of the guys are doing these days.

Everything about him radiates soldier. I wonder if he knows how intimidating he looks. And why the hell do I care what he thinks?

I'm going to be his tutor, not his shrink.

He shifts and his gaze collides with mine. Something tightens in the vicinity of my belly. It's not fear. Soldiers don't scare me, not even ones who look like they were forged in fire like Noah.

No, it's something else. Something tight and tense and distinctly distracting. I'm not in the mood for my hormones to overwhelm my common sense.

I stomp on the feeling viciously.

I'm staring at him now. I'm deliberately trying to look confident and confrontational. Men like Noah don't respect weakness. Show a moment's hesitation and the next thing you know they've got your ass pinned in a corner while they're trying to grab your tits.

He lifts one brow in response. I have no idea how to read that reaction.

Noah

I had to swallow my pride and ask some perky blond directions to The Grind. I hadn't expected Valley Girl airheadedness but then again, I didn't really know what I expected. I managed to interpret the directions between a few giggles and several "likes" and "ahs" and "ums". I imagined her briefing my CO and almost smiled at the train wreck it would be. We had a lieutenant like her once. She was in the intelligence shop and she might have been the smartest lieutenant in the brigade, but the way she talked made everyone think she was a complete space cadet.

She'd said "like" one too many times during a briefing to the division commander and yeah, well, last I heard, she'd been put in charge of keeping the latrines cleaned down in Kuwait. Which wasn't fair but then again, what in life was? Guess the meat eaters in the brigade hadn't wanted to listen to the Valley Girl give them intelligence reports on what the Kurdish Pesh and ISIS were up to at any given point in time.

My cup of coffee from The Grind isn't terrible. It certainly isn't Green Bean coffee, but it's a passable second place. Green Bean has enough caffeine in it to keep you up for two days straight. This stuff…it's softer, I guess. Smoother? I'm not really sure. It isn't bad. Just not what I'm used to. Nothing here is.

I wonder if there is any way to run down to Bragg and get some of the hard stuff. Hell, I am considering chewing on coffee beans at this point. Anything to clear the fog in my brain. But I need the fog to keep the anxiety at bay, so I guess I'm fucked there, too. Guess I should start getting used to things around here. No better place to start than with the coffee, I guess.

The Grind is busy. Small, low tables are crowded with laptops and books and students all looking intently at their work. It's like a morgue in here. Everyone is hyper-focused. Don't these people know how to have a good time? Relax a little bit? There are no seats anywhere. The Grind is apparently a popular if silent, place.

The tutor walks in at exactly twelve fifty-eight. Two minutes to spare.

"You're not late." I'm mildly shocked.

She does that eyebrow thing again, and I have to admit on her, it is pretty fucking sexy. "I tend to be punctual. It's a life skill."

"Kitty has claws," I say.

She stiffens. Apparently, the joke's fallen flat. Guess I'm going to have to work on that.

"Let's get something straight, shall we? My name is Beth, and I'm going to tutor you in business stats. We are not going to be friends or fuck buddies or anything else you might think of. I'm not 'Kitty' or any other pet name. I'm here to get a degree, not a husband."

My not-strong-enough coffee burns my tongue as her words sink in. She's damn sure prickly all right. I can't decide if I admire her spine or I think it's unnecessary. Hell, it isn't like I tried to grab her ass or asked her to suck my dick.

The coffee slides down my throat. "Glad we cleared that up," I say instead. "I wasn't sure if blowjobs came with the tutoring."

She grinds her teeth. There isn't much by way of

sense of humor in the tutor. She has a no-nonsense look about her. Her dark blond hair is drawn tight to her neck, and I can't figure out if she is naturally flawless or if she is just damn good with makeup.

There is a freshness to her, though, that isn't something I am used to either. Enlisted women, the few I've been around, either try way too hard with too much black eyeliner downrange or aren't interested in men beyond the buddy level.

But this academic woman is a new species entirely for me, and as our standoff continues, I realize I have no idea what the rules of engagement are with someone like her. At least not beyond her name is not Kitty and she's not here for a husband. Oh and can't forget the no blowjobs thing. She made the rules pretty clear.

She is fucking stunning and I suddenly can't talk.

She clears her throat. "So are we going to stand here and continue to stare at each other, or are we going to get to work? I have somewhere to be in two hours."

I motion toward the library. "Lead the way."

Beth

He's watching my ass as I walk in front of him. He's just the type who would do something like that. The blowjob comment caught me completely off guard. I hate that. I hate that I couldn't come up with any brilliant, sarcastic response, either. I always think of smartass comebacks fifteen minutes too late.

So now I am even more irritated than I was when he'd been staring at me class. What the hell had Professor Blake been thinking?

I lead us to a small table out of the way, where there won't be a lot of disruption. Stats is one of those things that takes a lot of concentration. At least it did for me until I learned the language.

I pull out the worksheet from class. Homework and lessons. "So let's get the business stuff out of the way," I say. I hate the tone in my voice. I'm not normally a ball-busting bitch, but he's set me off and if being cold and curt is the only way to keep him in line then so be it. "I'd like to be paid each meeting. Cash."

"What's your rate?"

I sit back. How the hell did that question catch me off guard? I don't know. I work part-time at the country club next to campus, but the tips are hit or miss. The thing about the wealthy? Some of them can be downright stingy. Most of the time, I make okay tips. When it isn't, I tried not to be bitter about how they don't need the money like I do.

I just smile and take their orders.

I'm stuck. Noah is not my first tutoring job, but my other jobs were paid for by the university. I have no idea how much to charge for freelance work.

"Fifty dollars an hour, three times a week," he offers abruptly.

I cover my shock with my hand. "Huh?"

"Fifty dollars an hour. I saw a sign in the common area charging that much for Spanish. Figure Stats should be at least that much, right?"

My voice is stuck somewhere in the bottom of my chest. Fifty bucks an hour is a lot of groceries and medication. It feels wrong taking that kind of money, even from Mr. Does-the-Tutoring-Come-with-Blowjobs.

"Will that be a problem?"

I shake my head. "No. That's fine." There's a stack of bills that need to be paid. The electricity is a week overdue. I'm counting on tips tonight to make a payment tomorrow to keep them from shutting it off. Again. Between that and the money from tutoring – I could keep the lights on. I can feel my face burning hot. I turn away, digging into my backpack to keep him from seeing my humiliation, not wanting him to see my relief.

"Same time, same place? Monday, Wednesday and Friday?" My computer flickers to life.

"Works for me. How much pain should I be prepared for?" He sounds worried. He should. Professor Blake is one of the top in her field, and that's no small feat considering she came up at a time when women were still blazing trails in the business world.

"Depends on if you do the work or not," I say. I can't quite bring myself to offer him comfort. I'm still irritated by the blowjob comment. "So let's get started." I lean over the worksheet. "What questions do you have from class today?"

I look up to find him watching me. There's something in his eyes that tugs at me. I don't want to be tugged at.

He looks away. He's strangling that poor pen in his hands. Clearly, I've struck a nerve with my question.

I wish I didn't remember how that felt. The lost sensation of not having a clue what I was doing. I didn't even know what questions to ask.

I don't want to feel anything charitable toward him, but there's something about the way he shifts. Something that makes him vulnerable.

I run my tongue over my teeth. This isn't going well. "Okay look. We'll start with the basics, okay?"

I open my laptop to the lecture notes.

He finally notices my computer. "I haven't seen one of the black MacBooks in years," he says.

He's not being a prick, but I bristle anyway. "It might be old but she's never failed me."

"It can run stats software? Isn't that pretty intense processor-wise?"

I don't feel like telling him that to run said stats program, I have to shut down every other program and clear the cache. I don't want to admit that there's just no money to buy a new computer. I can't even finance one because I don't have the credit for it.

Business school is about looking the part as much as it is about knowing the game, so none of those words are going to leave my lips.

"It gets the job done," I say. "Now, the first lecture."

"I get everything about what stats is supposed to do. I got lost somewhere around regression."

"Don't worry about regression right now. We're going to focus on understanding what we're looking at first up. Basic concepts."

I look over at him. He's scowling at the paper. I can see tiny flecks of gold in his dark brown eyes. He drags one hand through his short dark hair and leans forward. He's practically radiating tension, and I can feel it infecting me.

Damn it, I don't give a shit about his anxiety. I don't care. I can't.

"So the normal distribution is?"

I take a deep breath. This stuff I know. I draw the standard bell-shaped curve on his paper. "The normal distribution says that any results are normally…"

Noah

She knows her stuff. She relaxes when she starts talking about confidence intervals and normal distributions. Hell, I can't even *spell* normal distribution.

But she has a way of making things make sense.

And her confidence isn't scary so much as it is really fucking attractive.

I'm watching her lips move and I swear to God I'm trying to pay attention, but my brain decides to take a detour into not stats-ville. She's got a great mouth. It's a little too wide, and she has a tendency to chew on the inside of her lip when she's focusing.

I look down because I don't want her to catch me not paying attention. I need to understand this stuff, not stare at her like a lovesick private.

I'm focusing on confidence intervals when something dings on her computer. She frowns and opens her e-mail. It's angled away so I can't look over her shoulder, but something is clearly wrong. A flush creeps up her neck. She grinds her teeth when she's irritated. I tend to notice that in other people. I do the same thing when the anxiety starts taking hold. At least when it starts. It graduates quickly beyond teeth grinding into something more paralyzing.

I glance at my watch. It's almost time for her to go. I have no idea how I'm going to get my homework done, but I'll figure it out later. I'm meeting a couple of former military guys some place called Baywater Inn in a few hours. Plenty of time for me to get my homework done. Or at least attempt it. Because, of course, LT put me in touch with these guys, too.

But watching her, something is clearly wrong. I want to ask, but given how our history isn't exactly on the confide-your-darkest-secrets level, I don't.

She snaps her laptop closed and sighs. "I've got to run and make a phone call. Are you set for your assignment for lab?"

"I'll figure it out."

Her lips press into a flat line. "You can always

look it up online."

"Sure thing."

She's distracted now. Not paying attention. I watch her move. There's an edge to her seriousness now, a tension in the long lines of her neck. A strand of hair falls free from the knot and brushes her temple. I want to tuck it back into place, but I'm pretty sure if I tried it, I'd be rewarded with a knee in the balls. And I like them where they are, thanks. I've come too close to losing them to risk them now.

I pull out my wallet and hand her two twenties and a ten. She hesitates then offers the ten back. "We didn't do the full hour." I refuse the money. "Keep it. Obviously you've got something to take care of. Don't worry about it."

She sucks in a deep breath like she's going to argue but then clamps her mouth shut. "Thank you."

She didn't choke on it, but it's a close thing. I am suddenly deeply curious about what has gotten her all wound up in such a short amount of time.

Maybe I'll get a chance to ask her some day.

I definitely have the impression that Beth Lamont isn't into warm cuddles and hugs. She strikes me as independent and tough.

And I admire the hell out of that attitude, even as she scares the shit out of me with how smart she is.

About the Author

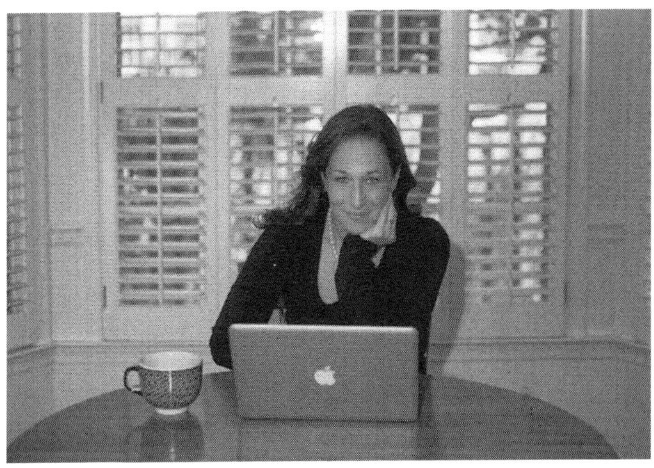

Jessica Scott is a career Army officer, mother of two daughters, three cats, and three dogs, wife to a career NCO, and wrangler of all things stuffed and fluffy. She is a terrible cook and even worse housekeeper, but she's a pretty good shot with her assigned weapon and someone liked some of the stuff she wrote. Somehow, her children are pretty well-adjusted and her husband still loves her, despite burned water and a messy house. No Zhu-Zhu Pets were harmed in the writing of this book.

Photo: Courtesy of Buzz Covington Photography

Also by Jessica Scott

HOMEFRONT SERIES

Come Home to Me
Homefront
After the War
Forged in Fire

FALLING SERIES

Before I Fall
Break My Fall
If I Fall

NONFICTION

To Iraq & Back: On War and Writing
The Long Way Home: One Mom's Journey Home From War

COMING HOME SERIES

Because of You
I'll Be Home For Christmas: A Coming Home Novella
Anything For You: A Coming Home Short Story
Back to You
Until There Was You
All for You
It's Always Been You